THE FLAWED ONES

Jay Chirino

ISBN: 0692928332
ISBN-13: 978-0692928332

To Samuel, for giving me the inspiration to learn, grow and face my biggest fears with courage.

FOLLOW THE MENTAL HEALTH MOVEMENT

Website:	Theflawedones.com/blog
Twitter:	Twitter.com/theflawedones
Facebook:	Facebook.com/theflawedones
Instagram:	Instagram.com/flawedones
National Alliance on Mental Illness:	Nami.org
National Suicide Prevention Lifeline:	1-800-273-8255

ACKNOWLEDGMENTS

I want to thank those people that not only believed in this project from the very start, but also encouraged me and took time to read, ponder and give me vital advice. Raquel, Elizabeth, Haty, thank you for your willingness to help and for buckling into this crazy ride. Mom and Dad, thank you for never doubting the man that I truly am. Mima, thank you for your relentless love.

PREFACE

Dear Reader,

Let me begin by saying that it is my absolute privilege to share this story with you. The fact that you will spend some of your precious time reading it means a great deal more to me than you will ever know. This is something very personal to me, something that I deeply connect with, something that in many respects I have lived. Writing this book took me the best part of twelve months, but in actuality, I have been writing it for close to thirty years. I have faced many serious challenges in my life, and several times I have felt defeated enough to want to fly the white flag. I am sure that you have felt like that from time to time, and it is that visceral connection all of us humans have that motivated me to write this story.

You see, our reality is shaped by our thoughts and what we surround ourselves with. When the sadness comes, our thoughts make us feel so alone that we begin to think we are the only ones in the world feeling that way. This is the reason we isolate and stay away from those that don't seem to comprehend, those people who tell us to "get over it" or "snap out of it." That is why we get drunk and high and we hurt ourselves, as a punishment for being so broken-- more broken than anyone else. My purpose with this book was not only to show you that we are all connected in some way, but also to prove to you how special every single one of us is, no matter how "broken" we think we are. For a while I had not been able to put into words what my true motive was for writing this book. I knew that I wanted a story that would move people, a story that many could relate with. But I still couldn't put my finger on it. Then, a few months back, someone asked me what I wanted most when I was going through my depression, and after thinking about it for a while, I figured it out. What I am trying to accomplish with this story is to help you see that you are not alone.

What you are about to read is fictional, but very real as well. It is a collection of events that may or may not have happened in some fashion or another. As it applies to me, yes, I am a recovering alcoholic and drug addict who spent over ten years destroying himself and the ones around him. Yes, I was hospitalized in psychiatric hospitals more than once, and I spent a long time trying to figure out what was wrong with me. My depression crippled me since I was a child, and without the right treatment or understanding, it made my life close to unbearable. My anxiety stopped me from living life, from enjoying the world, from seeing things in full color, and from chasing after my happiness. It was a very hard road to navigate, and one that I hope never to go through again.

The characters that you will meet in this story are a representation of the real struggles that a lot of us have gone through, and many of us still are. They are, sometimes, combinations of several people that I met in my journey. These people have meant a great deal to me, because they are the embodiment of the flawed human condition, the physical and mental glitches that affect us all in one way or the other. My intention by writing this story is not to paint anyone with any condition in a negative way; my purpose is to show you in some way how we are all the same, no matter what illness plagues us every single day. Our humanity supersedes any physical and mental blemish; love seems to flourish inside every one of us, one way or the other. I want you to take this into consideration when you think negative thoughts, or when you don't see the precious light at the end of the tunnel. We all must explore deep within ourselves and find the greatness that we all possess. Then we need to exploit that greatness and learn how to truly love ourselves. This will allow you to have a constant influx of love without the need of external sources. This, in my opinion, is the true way to happiness.

But I know this is easier said than done; heck, it took me over ten years to begin making progress, and I still have a long way to go. I do, however, want to tell you this, and if you feel the way I once did, I want you to bookmark this page so you can come back to it every time you need: You are not alone; you are not the failure that you think you are. You are not what other people want to convince you that you are. I know that it is hard, and I know that the strength to go on is sometimes fleeting, and it feels like it would be easier to give up. Easier, yes, worth it, no. Believe me. When you learn to see life the way you are supposed to see it, beautiful, with bad things and all, worth living, a privilege even, it will be a remarkable and extremely valuable experience. You are not alone; I cannot stress that enough. You are not the only one who does not see the colors of the world. I know how hard it can be to convince yourself of that. But your love is right there, deep inside you, not with the people who judge you and bully you and ignore you and play with your emotions. They are empty, and because they are empty they cannot share anything with you, because they don't have a thing to give. Don't feel sadness over the blind eyes that don't get to see the real you, or of the fearful hearts that would rather judge you and put you down so they don't have to deal with who they really are. Let your love and acceptance and uniqueness come from within you. Learn, little by little, to enjoy the things you like, for you and only you. Learn to see life through your eyes and no one else's. This, I promise you, will dramatically affect you in a positive way.

Is it just that easy? No, it isn't, unfortunately. Sometimes the chemicals in your brain will not let you progress the way you should. I am still tied to a daily dosage of medication, and let me tell you something, for that I feel really blessed. I feel fortunate that I was able to have an accurate diagnosis and to find something that could alleviate the pain just enough for me to be able to move forward. The medication is not an enemy; it is often necessary and it shouldn't make you feel ashamed. We all need a strong support system to succeed, and the meds are an important part of that equation. If you are one of those people who need them, like me, make sure that you stay on schedule and you take them the right way, and you will eventually see a dramatic impact on the way you feel.

If you are a family member or a caregiver of someone with an addiction problem or a mental illness, let me say, first and foremost, that you deserve a standing ovation for your strength, courage and everything you do for your loved one. Caregivers do not get the credit they deserve, yet they are there, fighting hard in the trenches every single day. I know that you too feel like giving up some days, and you might even feel guilty about thinking that way. Don't. You are an expression of overwhelming effort and sacrifice. You do what you do for love and responsibility, and the fulfillment of your duty makes you an exemplary human being, one that should be celebrated and acknowledged. You also are not alone. Many caregivers are fighting the battle every day, and managing it to see the good things through all the pain. I have such an admiration for people like you that it brings me to tears, tears of pride and deep respect. Thank you, thank you, and thank you again.

I hope this story touches you in some way and allows you to learn a little more about yourself. I hope that it makes you feel a little more understood, and that it gives you a little more hope for the future. Don't think that everything you are going to read will have a perfect ending. This is life we are talking about, not a fairy tale. But even through the sometimes dark and cruel reality, a beam of light seems to shine through, every time. Look for it, look for it within you and in the pages of this book. I promise you that you will not be disappointed if you do.

So, as I said before, what a privilege it is for me to share these words with you, to be right there, in your home, sharing something that I connect with so deeply, something that you may be able to relate with as well. It is my responsibility, however, to share what took so much time and pain and suffering to create, to make you laugh and make you cry, and give you hope, and for a moment, let you escape and connect with a version of your own self, encouraging you to find acceptance and hope, and love, all within you, as those things are already there.

I sincerely hope that is the case.

I live in constant conflict between my ambition and the awareness of the great futility of life.

CHAPTER 1

I was stained with the color of despair, my face as white as paper and my eyes afraid. I had not been me for a while and I didn't know how much destruction I had caused, but I had the terrible suspicion it had been a lot.

The room had nothing in it but a single-wide bed, right in the center. There were no pulse monitoring devices, blood pressure monitors or any other type of triage care equipment. Behind the bed was a window that brought in enough light to see that it was daytime, but it wouldn't be soon. There was a small television hanging from one of the walls, but it wasn't on. For a minute, the thought of looking for a remote ran through my mind, but just thinking about exerting that type of effort made me feel exhausted.

I sat in the middle of the bed, elbows resting on my knees and hands balled into fists, supporting my head. Mom and Dad stood next to me, pacing nervously in quiet desperation. They had not slept for days and their faces showed it. Their eyes told a story I didn't want to read, so I kept my head down and refused to make eye contact. There was a constant static noise inside my head that got gradually louder as the minutes went by, and by now it was getting to the point of unbearable. I tried squeezing my ears shut with my hands, closing my eyes and blowing out my nose, but nothing worked. It felt like the station inside my head had lost all reception, and only the white noise remained, slowly torturing me, forcing me to surrender the rest of my sanity.

A doctor eventually walked in the room, sporting a fake smile, as if its only purpose was to soothe me. It failed.

"Hello, my name is John, I am the ER doctor today," he said, still grinning without credible emotion. His whole expression had been programmed for dealing with the people he encountered, maybe in an attempt at making them more comfortable or at ease. He probably spent a long time in front of a mirror, perfecting it, practicing hard at masking his aversion to broken people, the reason he decided to become a doctor in the first place. Then he realized that fixing the broken meant being around them for a while, and he had no choice but to learn how to conceal his true feelings on the matter. I just hoped that his whole act worked better on others than it had on me.

"What brings you in today?"

His question was just part of the protocol; he already had the answer. His left hand had a grip on a chart that told him more than he needed to know, and I didn't have the desire to relive any of the details that had transpired the previous weeks. My blood would do that for me; it would give a thorough recount of the alcohol binge, the sedatives, the stimulants and whatever other substances I had put in my system without recollection. It would be a faithful witness of the events that made me lose total control and landed me in the hospital that day.

I kept it short and sweet to get things moving. "I have been struggling with depression and suicidal thoughts, self-medicating with alcohol and drugs," I said with embarrassment, not for telling the doctor, but for having to openly admit what I never had in front of my parents.

"I see…" Now the doctor's fake smile dissipated; my answer was the cue that gave him clearance to stop the pleasantries and get down to business. His new face was no better though; it had morphed into somewhat of a concerned frown, eyebrows making a considerable upward tilt where they ended, by his nose. His nostrils opened wider than normal, almost begging for more air. His eyes strained with focus as he made eye contact with nothing but the chart that he was writing on, while speaking to no one in particular.

"Let's go ahead and run some labs and see what medicine we can give you in the meantime, to ease some of the symptoms--deal?" He looked at me momentarily and there was one more artificial grin. Before I could nod in agreement he was walking out of the room, turning this time into his true, uninterested self. As he walked past the glass wall in front of me, I saw the real ER doctor for the first time. It almost made me feel relieved to not have to live with the lie, the clumsy act that he had to put on, just for me.

A needle went in my arm and painted three vials red. There went my story, no detail left behind. Questions were going to be asked, and truthful answers were going to be given. The dark era of lies and deceptions was finally coming to its inevitable end.

Then I waited, waited for help, a knot in my throat as the walls of the room started to close in. Sobriety sank, deep in my gut. I started reminiscing without anything to blur the images, and excruciating pain bubbled up inside me. There were projections on the walls, chopped up scenes of disastrous moments that defined the surrender of my sanity, of my happiness, of my hope. I wanted to scream, but didn't know how. I wanted to cry, but tears wouldn't come out. I sat still in the middle of the bed, and the walls were now so close that I could touch them with my hands. Mom and Dad became dark shadows that stood still in the background. The ringing in my ears became louder and it muffled everything else. My head started pounding harder than my heart, and my desolation became intolerable.

The wait continued, the minutes refusing to move on, time becoming relative to my discomfort. Mom and Dad still stood by my side. Their pacing had continued, just a little slower. Heads down, arms crossed, I could only imagine what was going through their heads. I was well aware of their exceptional distress and felt immense guilt knowing it was me who put it there.

Outside the room, movement continued. Nurses and doctors did their dance as stretchers drove by and parked in empty rooms, delivering their cargo. Green scrubs would rush to hook up monitors, get blood pressure readings and insert IVs. An agonizing patient begged for pain killers. The loudspeaker called out for a code blue in room twenty-six. Nurses sprinted past the room, almost in rehearsed formation.

I waited.

A blonde-haired woman now sat on a recliner on the other side of the glass wall, in front of the nurse's station. It seemed like she couldn't quite understand why she was there. She attempted to helplessly explain to the nurses and the cop standing by her that she had not meant to threaten anyone's life. It had just been a fit of anger, like the ones she had gotten before, during her first tries at sobriety. The nurses, with their empty smiles and careless eyes, nodded and ignored her. It wasn't a story they hadn't heard many times before, or one that could possibly change her outcome in any way.

Seventy-two-hour psychiatric hold. We were going to be staying on the same floor.

At last someone came. They had secured a room for me to stay in. My parents got close and embraced me. Mom gave me her "it's going to be ok" look, but the fear in her eyes said something else, something sadder. Dad walked past me and gave me two soft pats on the shoulder, then continued to walk out of the room, head down, as if my failures were his own.

As they disappeared into a corridor that now seemed five times longer than when we got there, my stomach ached the same way it did that very first day of public school, when they waved their hands in unison, and their blurry silhouettes shrank as I saw them vanish through the tears. I had never felt more alone, more abandoned. The complete weight and heat of my burning world rested entirely on my shoulders now. Would the elevator taking me to the third floor be able to hold that much? I was about to find out.

CHAPTER 2

He never looked at me, not once. At first, I thought that it was because he had repeatedly done the same thing with so many people that he had become numb to the procedure. I was just a package that needed to be safely transported from the first to the third floor, and he was the carrier.

But the more I studied him in an attempt at getting my mind off the indescribable pain, the more I realized that I was misjudging the man with the badge. There was a look in his eyes that told me there was a lot more going on than simple indifference. A lot more.

He was a black man with a bald head, his prime years now just stories that he would tell his grandchildren as they grew up. They would eagerly listen but not understand them at first, much less realize the reason he would tell them. Later, however, when things truly mattered, they would reminisce and find important lessons in each one, helping them navigate some of the unavoidable obstacles in life, metaphorically speaking, on their grandfather's back. By that time, the old man would be long gone, and he knew that, hence his reason for telling them so young.

Years of hardships and challenges had left him wise, but also scarred. Unnecessary wrinkles and bags under the eyes were clear evidence that the man with the badge had prioritized his work for many decades. It wasn't because he wanted to, but because his sense of responsibility compelled him to.

His eyes spoke in a way that his lips could not; they went back to places he'd rather forget. But those places were now tattooed in his pupils, and, in a sense, he liked it. It made him who he was, it gave him invaluable knowledge. Sometimes, however, he wished he could only be half the man he was if it meant erasing some of the memories. But memories are written in indelible ink, and pupils are crucial in order to see.

He walked past me and pressed the button to call for the elevator. He was a muscular man of six feet plus, with thick skin that shined as the lights bounced off it. His body towered over my thinner, shorter frame, and it made me feel a sense of intimidating respect. You could tell that back in his day, he would have had no problems picking the girl of his liking, as many went after him, his remarkable physique, his mystery, his quiet charm. He, however, only had eyes for one, *THE* one, and he didn't give up until he gave her his entire life. Out of all his regrets, that was never one.

He always looked forward and refused to make eye contact. The rhythm of his steps and the straightness of his back gave evidence of his military background. Maybe after a few tours on the other side of the world, fallen comrades, unspeakable atrocities and too many days away from his loved ones, he decided it was time to put on civilian clothes and ensure that people like me successfully made it to the third floor without hurting themselves or each other. It wasn't the highest paying or the easiest job sometimes, but it was honest and honorable. This man, you could tell, was all about honor.

Some of the habits you acquire in the military only die when you do. He was always very aware of his surroundings, and knew how to use his peripheral vision perfectly. Although he never made eye contact with me, he knew where I stood all the time, and I could tell he studied my body language in order to predict what I was going to do next. He learned this the hard way and promised himself never to get surprised again without being prepared.

The elevator dinged and opened its doors, like a mother opens her arms as she welcomes a young child. He extended his left arm and instructed me to jump in. I immediately obliged.

I stood in the back of the elevator as he stood with one hand on top of the other in front of the buttons, protecting them. The ride took less time than I thought, the elevator dinging once more and again opening its doors. The arm extended and prompted me to exit. He followed closely behind.

There was a short hallway that ended in a big double door. I walked until I could walk no more and waited for instructions. He came up and fiercely knocked on the door three times, then proceeded to again stand behind me, back erect, hand over the other, like a bouncer at the door of hell's night club.

A voice came from the other side of the door. "One second!" Steps followed and got louder as they approached. The door began to open.

The arm extended one last time and instructed me to make my way in. As I entered the darkness, I heard a deep yet surprisingly comforting voice.

"Son…"

I looked back and, for the first time, the man with the badge looked straight in my eyes.

"Best of luck to you."

I understood. It wasn't that he saw me as simple cargo; it was that he saw me as so much more, and this, he knew, was weakness, weakness he could not afford. Sometimes bigger hearts become easier targets, and his had been a bullseye too many times already.

The doors swung shut behind me, and a thought made me smile through the pain. The man with the badge will continue to do his work and do it well. How many great stories his grandchildren will be able to tell!

CHAPTER 3

At first glance the environment seemed chaotic, sometimes complete turmoil. For the most part, it was a loosely orchestrated play that featured multiple levels of mental illnesses, addictions, homelessness, crimes, suicide attempts, unspeakable loss and regrets--lots of regrets.

The young nurse who opened the door escorted me through the main corridor, past the lounge area and into a small exam room. As I walked by, I could feel eyes that followed me, some curious, others unaware. They just followed movement; it was the only thing they understood. Those empty stares brought shivers down my spine; they pierced like arrows through my skin, shattering bone and getting lodged deep inside me. Why did it feel like they could see through me better than anyone else?

As we made our way into the exam room, the blonde-haired woman I had seen downstairs made her way out. This time her face showed resignation; she had accepted the fact the she couldn't talk her way out of this particular situation. Outside she picked up an obscene amount of Prada luggage, obviously not packed with this stay in mind. Two nurses had to help her carry it. She walked in front of them, head held high, solemnly but with authority. One could tell that she had the knack for making people feel as if she owned them. She walked in her room and slammed the door shut after the nurses were done bringing in the luggage. A few moments later, a few desperate cries could be heard coming from the other side. *That's reality setting in*, I thought. *That is the most painful part of the whole procedure.*

The young man brought me in and asked me to sit on the exam table, then checked my vitals and close to every inch of my body, to ensure that I was not carrying any contraband. The room was cold and hard, crowded with medical equipment and the scent of iodoform. It was big enough for an intimate medical examination but too small for anyone with claustrophobia, or, as I have always referred to it, *moving walls syndrome*.

He then told me to remove my shoelaces and belt, proceeded to put them in a bag along with my wallet, and labeled it with my patient ID number. That property would be safely stored in a locker, away from suicidal hands.

After the ritual ended, he brought me out of the constricting little room and directed me to the general lounge area, which I later discovered was also the dining hall. There he told me to sit and wait until someone came for me. The plastic chair had metal armrests that felt crisp, like ice. The walls moved outwards this time, making everything and everyone distant. I found myself in the middle of nowhere, sitting on a frozen chair, in the dark. As the nurse walked away, a fear like the one I felt when my parents left the hospital was digging its claws in the most vulnerable parts of my soul.

The lounge/dining area stood in the middle. On each side were two corridors that spanned the length of the floor. Patient rooms were located on the outside of each hallway. Living quarters were explicitly basic: two single-wide beds, a small, empty shelf and a window with a sad view. The few restrooms that were available to patients had doors that didn't lock and shatterproof mirrors. If someone wanted to shave they would have to ask a nurse, and they would do it for them. Every precaution had been taken to avoid self-harm.

In front of where I sat was the nurse's station, a centralized location where all activity could be carefully monitored and analyzed.

There was always someone on the other side of the counter, pressing buttons on a keyboard. There was a surveillance office behind, where a guard could keep an eye on the entire floor through the security monitors. Behind me, on the wall, hung a clock that at first glance seemed to be broken. I later realized that there was nothing wrong with it; it was time itself that was broken inside these walls.

It didn't take long to notice that a new face brought lots of attention. As I sat there, an array of looks consistently headed my way. They were concerned, confused, threatened and angry looks. For the most part, however, a lot of the patients seemed eager to make new friends. It meant having new ears to tell their story to, the story that no one there wanted to hear again, the record that had been overplayed a long time ago.

Regardless of how they felt about new tenants, most of the patients were lucid enough to understand that not everyone that walked through the doors would be friendly, much less polite. They had to wait and see how the newcomers were going to act, and that would dictate how close they were going to get. After a couple of days, maybe, they could plan a prudent approach.

There were several types of individuals roaming the halls, entering and exiting their rooms, coexisting in the most dysfunctional of ways. Some of them wore hospital gowns that were wrinkled and dirty, barely hanging on as they moved about. They wore them for several days in a row, and the stench of their unbathed bodies was cruel to the senses. They walked at slower than normal speed most of the time; the world did not move as fast for them as it did for others. There was an eerie emptiness in their eyes, most likely a combination of their illness and the strong medication, and they roamed the halls as soulless bodies that had no motivations, intentions or ambitions. They existed on the most desolate plane of reality, right before death. I nicknamed them zombies, although I felt guilty thinking of them that way.

In contrast, others paced as if they were late for the most important meeting of their lives, making unnatural gestures with their hands and talking out loud to themselves. The world they were living in was simply not the same; it was an alternate dimension that only they had access to, and only their broken minds could understand. Sometimes, out of the blue, they would scream profanities or make bizarre statements that only made sense to them. They yelled about government conspiracies and plots to get them killed, demons and angry gods, vengeful children who would follow them around and secret societies they were a part of. Sometimes I wondered if they knew something that the rest of us didn't. More than once I witnessed nurses having to forcefully hold them down and give them shots, as they had a hard time taking their medications willingly. Big bruises would be left on their arms and legs due to their muscles being so tense at the time of injection. Seconds later, gears downshifted and their world would slow down, maybe a little too much now. The quick pacing and loud talking would stop, the soul left the body and for a few minutes, maybe hours, a zombie was born.

There were those who, like me, were there for other, not-so-obvious reasons, like addictions, run-ins with the law, violent outbursts, death threats, suicide attempts. Family members would sometimes be left without a choice; they would have to call the authorities and put their loved ones under an involuntary psychiatric hold. Those who tried to take their own lives had to be carefully monitored and wore a red bracelet around their wrist. The patients who seemed relatively normal were the ones that scared me most, as I couldn't figure out what they were capable of. I'm sure that for the same reason they were cautious of me as well.

As I sat in front of the broken clock, movement never ceased. Zombies would slowly approach and get a whiff of my scent (as I would unwillingly get one of theirs), then walk away when they perceived that I wasn't a threat. Others would sit on the lounge and draw, or write long essays, or play with cards, table games and puzzles. Some would just sit and explore their worlds, the ones inside their heads, while reality became a distant, unreachable star that they were most likely unaware existed. Some gathered small crowds and preached about the end of the world, the Illuminati and the secret spaceships hovering above Earth, waiting to extract and dispose of the weaker ones. Needless to say, having an audience that mostly consisted of listeners with severe anxiety and extreme paranoia, these kinds of topics could cause plenty of unrest.

Sometimes, in the distance, loud screams would be heard, and punches to walls so hard that they'd resonate in your chest, followed by more terrified screams. A few trained nurses would sprint to the scene and the situation would be, most of the time, quickly contained. Other times guards had to get involved and restraints had to be used. In order to do that, however, the hospital had to call the patient's family and get prior permission to avoid facing legal repercussions in the future. If they didn't have any family, they would have to involve the state.

The higher functioning individuals, which I later nicknamed *the lucid*, seemed to mostly gather in the TV room on the other side of the hall. It was the safest place, away from the madness and incoherence of the others, but not always tranquil. From time to time one could hear scuffles about whose turn it was to control the remote, or what channel to put on. A nurse or two would always be close by to ensure things didn't turn violent, but they weren't always in time.

As I continued to wait, a disheveled woman with crooked eyes and a very abnormal limp walked past me, crying. As she roamed the floor without purpose, she would look back into the emptiness of the dim-lighted hall and yell with dismay, "Please! I beg you! Stop laughing at me! OH GOD!" I momentarily focused on this woman and peered into her eyes for as long as I could stand it, long enough to see what she saw, and to understand how real it was for her. It was a nightmare that had no end, a horror that could not be escaped. As she walked away in panic, the frigidity of her fears crawled inside me, and for a few seconds I understood the ravenous terror of constant torment.

After a while, a nurse approached me and let me know that I was now able to go into my room and settle in. I would see Dr. Patel in the morning. In the meantime, they would give me a light sedative to help me sleep. *A light sedative is definitely not going to do it*, I thought, as there was no way I would be shutting both of my eyes at the same time in this place.

The nurse gave me a flimsy toothbrush, a small toothpaste tube and a hairbrush, then told me to go into room 217 and put everything on the shelf closest to the second bed, the one by the window. As I walked in, a short, stubby man of maybe forty was making his way out. He was bald and had a goatee that reminded me of a biker dude from the nineties. He took a meticulous look at me, extended his hand and said, "What's up, man? I'm Jerry. Looks like we are going to be roommates tonight. I really hope you don't pee yourself. I slept bathed in the stench of piss last night. Jesus..."

I was at a loss for words for momentarily. "I'm Jay, and no, I don't pee myself at night--at least I don't think so," I finally replied.

Jerry smirked. He must have seen the fear in my face and immediately felt a sense of empathy toward me. "Don't worry, kid, it could be worse. I leave tomorrow but before I do I'll make sure to point out a few friends for you."

"I appreciate that, Jerry," I said with some relief.

"No worries..." he said, and then a light bulb came on in his head. "Oh, and another thing, and this one is important, trust me... Stay away from the little one..."

CHAPTER 4

I lay on my back with eyes open, staring at the ceiling as Jerry's snores filled the air with vexatious rhythm. He had no problem falling fast asleep, but as I expected, no "light sedative" was going to knock me out tonight.

It wasn't only the fear, the anxiety and the relentless thoughts that were keeping me awake. Every fifteen minutes or so a nurse would barge into the room, momentarily shine a bright light in our faces and walk away as she made a checkmark on a clipboard. I guess they could not give us enough time alone to succeed in killing ourselves or each other, so instead they robbed us of whatever soundness of mind we had left.

The air conditioning unit by the window competed with Jerry's snores as to who could be the loudest, and yet the night seemed eerily quiet, so quiet that my thoughts became more persistent than usual, in a desperate attempt to break the silence. Thoughts that I had been trying to keep out of reach for a while started to appear loud and clear, and I had no access to any substance that would quiet them down. The images formed in high definition and refused to be turned off. I was chained to my subconscious and forced to watch the show.

I saw her face, smiling with that smile that made my knees weak and my heart tremble with a rush of emotion. She connected with my eyes and got lost in hopes and dreams, in plans of a future with good food, far travels, of kisses under the rain and cuddles on those cold nights, where the air smells of wood fire and the breeze turns your cheeks red. In me she saw her every day; getting home from work to a cup of coffee and destressing conversation, walks under autumn leaves and sunsets in the summer. She saw a confidant who would never let her down, a friend she could always trust, a lover who would always satisfy her. I could tell by the way she looked at me that with me she saw eternity in her finite existence, death not a worthy adversary against the strength of our love.

The scene in my head abruptly changed, and now there I was, sitting in a bed, forcing an exorbitant number of pills down my throat, coming in and out of consciousness, every memory a choppy blur. I heard yelling in the distance but couldn't tell where it was coming from. I could feel the force of someone rocking me back and forth-- maybe an effort to make me listen, to pay attention. But it wasn't working; I became nauseous and more belligerent. Another change of scene and there she was, in the corner of a dark room, sitting on the floor with knees bent toward her face, sobbing uncontrollably, shaking in her own sweat. All her face now showed was unmeasurable fear and emptiness, a deep black hole in the middle of her soul that gradually expanded and swallowed every dream it touched, leaving her with nothing but flagrant dismay.

Another abrupt change of scene and she smiled again, hope radiating one more time, eyes shining with revived expectations. I remembered that expression, I yearned for it, as it tugged my insides with more force than anything in existence. For a second it made me happy and brought me a smidgeon of comfort, but the feeling didn't last long, as I was forced to pay attention and figure out the reason for her glow. She took off her clothes, slowly, with that raw sensuality that was as unique to her as her signature. Her top came off and so did her skirt, leaving her in nothing but her pink underwear, the ones from Victoria's Secret that I had bought and surprised her with on our first anniversary. She almost looked shy, as if she was about to reveal a very deep secret, one she never had. Her bra found its way to the floor, and her breasts looked as splendid as ever, gleaming in the soft lights, bathed in her unblemished alabaster skin.

A pair of masculine hands grabbed her firmly by her waist, and she sighed with lust. The tip of the fingers traveled north, barely touching her skin, just enough to drive her crazy. Her eyes rolled back and her mouth stayed open but did not make a sound. She was in so much pleasure she was forgetting to breathe. His mouth found hers and nibbled on her lower lip, as his hands now held both of her breasts tightly. He passionately pushed her onto the bed and climbed on her, without losing contact with her mouth. Two bodies started to tumble and intertwine, two bodies started to become one. The rest of her underwear quickly came off; she wasn't shy about sharing her secret anymore. She closed her eyes and tried to hold her moans but didn't succeed. Sweat gushed from her pores and she glistened. Her neck arched as she let out a loud, extended sigh that signaled her climax. Then she breathed heavily, full of satisfaction, as she looked in the eyes of the man who had brought her inexplicable pleasure, a man who wasn't me.

My body automatically sat up in the bed and a loud scream came out of the deepest parts of my spirit. I screamed for as long as I had air in my lungs, and when I stopped to catch my breath, I realized I had screamed with so much force that my ribs felt bruised and my throat was sore. A horrific panic began to penetrate my skin, making me tingle everywhere. My accelerated breathing was making me wheeze uncontrollably, and my heart rate was dangerously fast.

Jerry did not move a muscle; his snores continued battling the air conditioning for dominance. The door opened and the light hit my face, this time for a few seconds longer, to make sure I was ok. A check mark was made and the quiet darkness showed up again.

I laid back down on the bed, afraid to close my eyes. I did not want to relive another scene like that. But that raw emotion could not be concealed with alcohol or drugs any more. I was tethered to the clarity of my mind, and it wanted to express itself thoroughly now that it had my full attention. I begged, *Please! Don't let me see this again, please!*

No one was listening.

Over and over my mind replayed a moment in time that I had not been present for, and with every playback my desperation grew larger. *Please! Make it stop, please!* Tears fell down my face and my body shook ferociously, my heart palpitated and I could not catch my breath. The only answers I got, however, where from Jerry's snores and an air conditioning unit that persisted in making the room much colder that it should have been.

Finally, exhausted and defeated, I allowed myself to sleep for a few minutes, but it wasn't long before another flash of light woke me up, a check mark was made on the clipboard, and torturing thoughts started to plague me again. *Funny,* I thought in my agony. Since I had gotten here I had been afraid of the ones out there, roaming the halls. Little did I know that the real source of horror was inside my head, and it could not be escaped.

That thought made me chuckle at first, and then made me break into maniacal laughter that went on for several minutes. I was losing my mind in the very place that was supposed to save it.

Jerry continued to snore, unscathed and oblivious. How could he sleep amidst all this commotion?

He is leaving tomorrow. He's been bathed in piss and God only knows what else. To Jerry, this is the most peaceful night he's had in this God-forsaken place.

CHAPTER 5

It was probably around four-thirty in the morning when my body, finally exhausted, forced my mind to shut down and allowed me to rest. Not long had passed when the lights in the room abruptly came to life and obnoxiously burned my eyes.

"Checking vitals, fellas," said the nurse as she walked in with a portable blood pressure monitor and heart rate indicator. She looked as annoyed to be there as I was. I could only imagine how many vile things she'd already heard that morning, waking up highly dysfunctional and medicated individuals so early.

She had acquired thick skin throughout the years though, and the skill of letting things roll off her back with ease. To her, it was a matter of speed. How long would it take her to walk in and out of a room to get the job done? She probably timed herself and worked hard to beat her best time, and her level of exasperation would diminish if she was able to improve it. Everyone needs an anchor to let the grueling hours of the day pass by a little quicker.

Jerry was closest to the door, so he was first up. Incredibly, he didn't seem at all bothered; his snores never went out of rhythm. An arm lifted from under the sheets and waited for the blood pressure cuff to wrap around it. The machine started breathing air into the cuff and a few seconds later began to exhale. It finalized by making three fast beeps that signaled a reading. The nurse quickly wrote it down and rolled the equipment to my side of the bed.

The whole procedure did not take more than five minutes, but it felt like an hour to me. Through the bright lights, I could only see a blurred silhouette in front of me, feeling the pressure of the cuff as it hugged my arm. Once the lights in the room were off again, I felt so exhausted that I was happy at the prospect of closing my bloodshot eyes and getting some sleep. It was now all I wanted, to just sleep for a while, no tormenting thoughts, blinding lights or medical tools, or heavy snores, or freezing temperatures.

Just pure, unadulterated sleep.

This time it felt like I got some decent shut-eye for a bit longer than before. When the door of the room slammed open, a hint of sunlight was already peeking through the window, warming it up significantly. Jerry was no longer in the room, leaving me to fend for myself in the situation that was about to ensue.

I sat up in the bed and rubbed my eyes vigorously to ensure that what I was seeing was real. A young woman had barged in and was now standing against the wall, one hand on her chest, hyperventilating.

"Oh my God, oh my God, oh... my God!" she whispered repeatedly at such speed that it sounded like her words were all one. Her chest would inflate and deflate strenuously, trying to keep up with the oxygen demand.

"Are you... ok?" I said, in the most soothing tone I could possibly find in such an unnerving situation.

"A man, a gargantuan man, had a huge anger episode and ripped the entire phone box off the wall," she said, her chest still bouncing up and down like a basketball.

"Please help me, I'm scared!" Her eyes began to moisten and tears appeared. "I didn't know what to do. All the nurses ran past me to hold him down and give him a shot. There were five or six of them and they still couldn't hold him down! It happened next to my room and they were blocking the door. I couldn't go past them to get inside, I didn't know what to do…" The tears began to flow like a waterfall. "I'm so scared!" She balled up the hand she had against her chest into a fist and pressed it hard against her, closing her eyes briskly, as if trying to make her fear go away with the power of her mind.

"Just… calm down. You are safe here, nothing to worry about anymore," I said to her, but in reality, I was trying to reassure myself.

She was a young woman, no more than five feet tall. She wore thick glasses that magnified her eyes to twice their normal size, and had pale skin that had not seen the light of day in quite some time. She was a little heavyset, but not overweight, and unlike most patients, she wasn't wearing a hospital gown. Her blouse had quite the colorful flower arrangement on it, and her jeans went too high up her waist. Her fears were honest and pure; you could tell she could not hide her emotions, not like the rest of us could.

I got out of bed, slowly, trying to not frighten her more. I stood by her for a few seconds and with loosely calculated precision wrapped my hands around her shoulders in a risky attempt at comforting her.

She gradually nuzzled her way into my chest and just stood there for a while, in uncomfortable silence. I could now feel her heartbeat ricocheting vigorously against me. After a couple of minutes, I looked down to notice her head tilting up to make eye contact with me. Her heartbeat dissipated and retreated to an almost normal pace.

As soon as her eyes locked into position with mine, the expression of fear that was written on her face instantly vanished, as if a magician had tapped her in the head with a wand, or as if a hacker had deleted all the bad thoughts and fears from her hard drive. I was now in the presence of a completely different person.

Her big eyes squinted and her mouth formed a smile. She now reminded me of a five-year-old girl who was just given a reward for good behavior. "Hi, I'm Tara, nice to meet ya!" She hugged me by the waist and put her ear to my chest as if trying to decipher what was ticking in there. She then squeezed me hard enough for me to let out an audible gasp, and for my already sore ribs to hurt even more.

Without warning she released me from her grip and began skipping out the door as Jerry was walking in. It was almost like she had experienced some sort of amnesia and could not remember the events that had transpired just a few minutes before.

Jerry looked back, petrified, as she made her way out. He looked at me, then back at her and back at me again, startled and confused. Maybe it was because he knew the rules; male patients could not cohabitate with female patients in the rooms. Maybe it was something else.

"What... the hell... was the little one doing in here?" he asked, almost rhetorically.

I chuckled at first, and then, when I saw the look on Jerry's face, got rather scared.

What the hell indeed.

CHAPTER 6

"I was born an anxious kid, with fear a loyal companion every step I took. Growing up an only child with overprotective parents meant that I was shielded from really learning how to fend for myself out there, in the real world.

"I wore concealer on my face my first day of school, not as a fashion statement, but because I cried so much that morning that Mom had to plaster it on me, in a desperate attempt at hiding my swollen eyes and red cheeks. The thought of being all alone in a place full of strangers, without anyone to hold on to for emotional support and protection, wasn't just scary; it was downright terrifying.

"I remember that the old fan in the corner of my bedroom had metal blades and an electric motor that looked like it previously belonged to some type of landscaping tool, maybe an edger or a weed whacker. It was connected to a hollow metal tube that ended attached to an old wheel, which served as base. The whole thing had been spray painted gray, adding to its already industrial look. My late grandfather had put it together years before my birth, and it was considered as much a member of the family as any other of his inventions.

"In order to turn on the fan, you had to manually spin the blades clockwise (so they would turn in the right direction) and switch on the motor. When it finally came to life, it made a noise like that of a small plane, and it probably generated as much thrust. Aside from the loud noise and the risk of losing a limb if you got too close to it, the fan was a great piece of machinery. On those scorching nights filled with humidity, having the metal giant watching over you and cooling your sheets was a luxury. And one would get so used to the noise it made that after a while it would be difficult to sleep without it.

"Mom's morning routine included making breakfast and coffee, mopping the floor, preparing lunch and eventually shutting the fan off to get me ready for school. It was the slow decline of the blades, the disappearing noise and the dissipation of wind flow that would make me wake up every morning, promptly reminding me that it was time to start the dreadful routine.

"My heart palpitated and sweat would engulf my hands as I got out of bed and headed to the bathroom. My eyes would start swelling with tears, and my stomach would curl more than a yoga instructor as I brushed my teeth with little strength. Mom would eventually have to remind me how everyone noticed the makeup that first day of school. It would be a shame if we had to remind them of that unfortunate occasion again. So I would have to do my best to swallow my fear and suck in the tears, get dressed and ready for another day of hell and just do my best to get through it. Some days it was harder than others. Back then the teachers taught on a fear-based system and had no qualms about punishing children in sometimes extreme and sadistic ways. Many parents even gave them authority to physically hit their kids if they misbehaved. Even though I never got in trouble, witnessing the things they did to others in the classroom mortified me. I still remember the screams of third graders getting hit repeatedly on the back of the legs with plastic rulers, or sitting on the floor for extended periods of time with bottlecaps under their knees. Dealing with other children was no picnic either, and I was repulsed by the anxiety that the whole ordeal gave me. I would have done anything never to feel it again.

"Every morning the fan would die off and the routine would play over. My heart rate would elevate, tears would start to form and Mom had to once again give me the makeup pep talk. Then came the long walk to school that felt as if I was heading to an instant death by firing squad.

"I would eventually make it to class, and initially things were never as bad as I had seen them in my head. But not being socially adept to handle myself with confidence resulted in eventually becoming an outcast, getting bullied and occasionally tormented. I cringe every time I hear about the purity and innocence of young children, about the light in their eyes and the goodness that must be protected. As far as I remember, it is at a very young age when the human race is truly at its most honest, jealous, ignorant and cruel. I don't think most parents see that though, and they do absolutely nothing to positively influence their children's behavior. This leads them to grow up not knowing how to be decent members of society.

"I was greeted with occasional beatings, because everyone knew that the quiet, weird kid was not going to retaliate, and what eight-year-old doesn't need a live punching bag to practice on? I never got shoved into any lockers, for the mere reason that there weren't any at my school; otherwise, I'm sure that I would have gotten very familiar with their interior architecture. I did, however, get pushed into concrete walls and kicked to the floor from time to time, which makes me wonder if the locker thing would have been a bad thing after all.

"Alexis always seemed to have a special interest in me; only God knew why. He had a repertoire of *funny skits* he liked to show off to the class, with me as his unwilling assistant. I would usually end up bruised up, written on, half naked and crying, to the amusement of Alexis' audience. He was by far the shortest kid in the school, and I concluded that he picked on me to take the attention away from his tiny stature. I began to convince myself that I was doing a good deed by helping Alexis not get bullied himself, and for that I should feel proud. But feeling proud of being the school's buffoon was not the easiest thing to do.

"I was nine years old when I experienced my first depressive episode.

"A lot of people describe depression as a void that swallows you whole and won't let you feel anything at all. My depression consisted of immeasurable sadness that depleted any positive feeling or outlook for the future. It was a black hole that attracted and swallowed my reasons for being happy, the things that I enjoyed doing, the desire to do anything at all. I didn't feel like dying, but I didn't feel like living either. I was alive only because my lungs still breathed oxygen and my heart pumped blood through my veins. Little did I know at the time that a nine-year-old should not be feeling such an overwhelming emptiness, but I was, in ways that were almost impossible to accurately explain. I also became occasionally paranoid; some nights I would be terrified of closing my eyes, fearing that the darkness would seep through them and when I opened them in the morning I would be blind. I convinced myself that I would eventually die in my sleep, and not being aware of the transition from life to death would make me panic. There were other times where I would notice my parents acting in ways that to me went against their character, so I became suspicious that they weren't really my parents, but imposters who took their place.

"I woke up one morning and the world had turned a shade of gray that lacked life, enthusiasm and most of all, hope. The fan came to a stop that day and I could not find the strength to get out of bed, much less argue my decision of not going anywhere.

"Mom must have noticed the change, as she didn't even argue or attempt the makeup pep talk when I told her I was staying home. She looked at me, concerned and intrigued, nodded and cranked the fan back on, then stood in silence by the door, studying me. She walked away, head down, when she couldn't find the answer she was looking for.

"Three days went by and her concern transformed into worry when she saw that my condition had not improved. Now she and Dad would constantly hover over the bed, asking the same questions over and over again: *Why are you so down? Can you tell us what's wrong? How can we help?*

"The answer was always the same: *I don't know.*

"To me, the world had lost its reason for spinning. Putting one foot in front of the other and getting out of bed was pointless. It was a feeling of constant falling into a bottomless abyss without knowing how to fly or make myself wake up from the nightmare. I lost my sense of self and started questioning my own reality. I spent days bathed in sadness and nothing else. My hygiene became so bad that Mom had to give me sponge baths and brush my teeth in bed, as I lay there, slightly more alive than dead.

"I struggled with the idea of purpose, as I became convinced there wasn't any.

"My parents were obviously very worried and tried to help in any way they could, but failed miserably. Living under religious and cultural stigma left them with hands tied and an ignorance that was hard to overcome. Taking someone (especially a child) to a psychiatrist or even a psychologist was reserved for the mentally ill and psychotic, not the melancholic. So they resorted to the only thing they knew: prayer, Bible passage readings, visits and pep talks from the congregation leaders and the occasional *"you need to get it together and snap out of it; you are stronger than this"* that made me feel even lonelier, as it was proof that no one really understood what I was going through.

"Several weeks went by and not much changed. I continued lying in a stupor of sadness as the Earth rotated and the days passed, until one fateful morning. The old fan came to a stop and the sun came through the window, and I found myself very interested in the specks of dust that danced in the light right above me. *It's like they move in certain patterns, almost relative to each other*, I thought. *It's like they dance with each other and know what the next move should be before they do it. Could dust specks have a gravitational pull? Do they attract each other like galaxies attract each other in space? Do galaxies move like dust specks, or do dust specks move like galaxies?*

"It took me a minute to realize something had changed. It wasn't only that the sun was shining a little brighter that day; it was also that something caught my attention, something had interested me enough to make me think, to make me wonder. A thought that wasn't sad or anxious had crept in without me even noticing, and it was virally creating other interesting thoughts that were, for the first time in a while, not full of gloom.

"I smiled.

"I was feeling slightly better. Things didn't change overnight, but gradually; it was a slow process. I started getting out of bed more often, hygiene improved and the world got some of its pizzazz back. "Eventually I got tired of being a bum all day and decided it was time to incorporate myself to reality again, as challenging as I knew that would be. But my brain begged for stimulation, it wanted to go out there and learn and be challenged, and I knew that wasn't going to happen staying at home.

"I was honest with my parents and told them about the challenges I was facing in school. They decided it was time for a fresh start and moved me to another campus, where they made sure to thoroughly explain to the teachers my situation and worked closely with them to monitor me both at home and in class. Things got a little better after that, and for a while I enjoyed my studies and got somewhat closer to some of my classmates.

"I wish I could say that this was my first and last depressive episode, but I would be lying if I did. My life has been deeply affected by these bouts of sadness. Things got truly worse when alcohol entered the picture and I..."

"Let's stop there for today," Dr. Patel said, while dotting her I's and crossing her T's on the chart.

"Well Jay, it seems like we are dealing with a depressive disorder that could potentially be manic, or bipolar. There is some childhood trauma that we must work through and try to reconcile as well. I don't have enough data to make an accurate diagnosis yet; we've just began the process, but I think we are off to a good start. Let's put you on the right meds to get you feeling better and we will continue this exploration tomorrow. I am prescribing 75 mg of Effexor in the morning and 100 mg of Seroquel at night. Let's see how that works and we shall go from there."

"How about for the, um, the anxiety?" I asked, hoping to God that I could get some kind of benzo out of her.

"Well..." She sighed and looked down at the chart. "I want to see how you do without benzodiazepines for a while, since you have had problems with them recently. We will keep an eye on you and if you exhibit any withdrawal symptoms we will taper you off, but for now let's try going this this route."

Dammit. I nodded in agreement; it was not as if I had a choice in the matter, but it was worth a shot.

As I walked out of the office, for some reason, the thought of the old metal fan remained in my head. We had left our home and country 20 years ago, but the old fan stayed behind. I wondered if it was still cooling the sheets of some kid's bed, while providing the loud yet soothing noise of the metal blades and the weed whacker motor to break the silence of the night. I wondered if its morning demise was still letting some anxious kid know that it was time to get up and face a scary world, today, hopefully, without any makeup on.

CHAPTER 7

It was almost time for Jerry to leave the joint and he had gathered, like a superstar, a small group of fans outside the room, waiting eagerly to say their goodbyes.

"They are all God's children," Jerry would say, and he meant it. During breakfast that morning, he ran around making sure the patients who had a hard time eating were out of bed and sitting at a table. He helped the nurses distribute the trays and would personally deliver some of them to his "low appetite" friends, to make them accountable for not refusing his food. He then sat down with Oliver, who was almost completely blind, and spoon fed the old man while sharing war stories. Out of the many things they had in common, the Marine Corps was the main one. Oliver's murky eyes would glisten as he listened to Jerry talk, and from time to time he would let out a faint but honest laugh that would make Jerry smile.

That day when the plate was empty and Jerry stood up to go return the tray, he felt Oliver's hand feeling around his upper arm, attempting to connect with his. When the blind man finally succeeded, he squeezed hard and held Jerry's hand for a while, lost in the darkness that was now his entire world. Neither Oliver or Jerry spoke; they just stayed there, motionless, saying with their silence what they couldn't say with their words. They understood each other almost telepathically, their trajectories in life not having been so different. Jerry knew that out of everyone in the entire world, Oliver was the one who saw him best. He finally tapped the old man on the shoulder a couple of times, discreetly wiped a few tears from his face and moved on to Tara, who was refusing to eat, as she was convinced that her bagel was poisoned.

I didn't quite hear what he whispered in Tara's ear, but it worked. She instantly, although still wary, took a few bites from her bagel, cautiously looking over her shoulder to make sure that she would not be attacked from behind while she was focused on her food, distracted.

Afterwards Jerry had briefly met with his social worker to discuss his departure, and after a few minutes of what looked like upsetting conversation, he ran into the room, visibly distraught. I discreetly walked in behind him, first to make sure that he was ok and offer my assistance, secondly because being out there, without him close, was still somewhat terrifying.

We found ourselves both lying in our beds, looking at the ceiling with our hands on our heads. We looked more like teenagers resting in a field of grass on a summer night, trying to keep track of all the falling stars that followed their path to only-God-knew where, or why. The confinement of the psychiatric floor disappeared momentarily, and we felt not only free, but a bit more alive. It was the intrinsic connection that I had created with Jerry that made me feel safe around him, knowing that he sincerely had my best interest in mind, and for a few seconds, I felt a hint of peace. Jerry was still distraught over his meeting with the social worker, and after a few minutes of silence, he decided to break it.

"I risked my life for this country, you know, some would say courageously, and this is what I get." He turned his head and looked at me. "Do you know why I'm here, Jay?"

I shook my head. "No Jerry, I don't. For a minute this morning I thought you were an undercover nurse!" The thought brought a laugh to both of our faces, then there was momentary silence again.

"Three tours in Iraq scarred me, deep. I've never talked about it, not even to the doctors. They say I need to process the feelings and the pain, you know, but I'm too macho for that. It's bullshit; we ain't nothing but flesh and bones waiting for their turn to rot. The images of the field of battle..." he paused, "...they're stamped in the back of my head--superglued, I should probably say. I lost friends, good men, good fathers, and sons, and husbands. I saw them bleed out; I carried their severed limbs and their bodies, mutilated by shrapnel. Some died in front of me, a few of them in my arms even. You don't know, Jay, you just don't know what it's like to feel that helpless. Sometimes I wish it had been me, I wish I would've been the one laying in someone's arms, ready to finally meet my maker and be accountable for what I've done. Sometimes I feel selfish for thinking that way. I came home tired, defeated. I had lost my purpose, I misunderstood the reasons that led me to become a soldier. I could not figure out why I decided to fight for our freedom, choosing to imprison my mind in the gates of hell instead. I was physically home now, but mentally, I was still at war. If I went shopping or to the gas station, or for a walk in the park with my wife, the enemy was always there, stalking me, waiting for the right time to strike. I was in defensive mode all the time; my instincts were misleading me constantly. I got lost inside the fear in my head, and couldn't find a way out.

"My paranoia led me to carry a gun everywhere, even to bed. Sometimes the nightmares would wake me up and I would draw it in the shadows, pointing it at the silhouettes that I saw running toward me, not realizing there was nothing there. The gun went off a couple of times, and I thank God to this day that no one was hurt. I started drinking occasionally, just to, you know, try to get away. The fights at home became more frequent, more violent, and I... I did things that I greatly regret. My wife became scared for her life because of my erratic behavior, so she took our twelve-year-old son and moved to Orlando with her mother.

"It was after the restraining order and losing my house, the right to see my kid and my dignity as a human being that alcohol took a complete hold of me, and I now found myself fighting the demons inside my head while begging on the streets for my next forty..." He smirked sarcastically. "A decorated soldier, national hero, begging on the streets... It's the only thing that quiets them, Jay, the only thing."

"I know the feeling, Jerry," I said, feeling a great deal of empathy for the man.

Jerry tried to change the tone. "So every once in a while, when I get tired of the streets and the crowded shelters, and when I need a refill on the meds I barely take, I make the VA pay for a few days here, just so I can get a decent night's sleep."

"Your son?" I asked.

"All grown up," he answered. "Married, two kids, a much better father than I ever was. Social worker called him this morning to see if he could take me in for a while. He refused, so I guess it's back to the streets for me, kiddo. See, I told you, this ain't so bad!" He smiled and continued gazing at the shooting stars for a little while longer, but reality was already bringing the ceiling back to its original place. We both knew we had very little freedom left.

"I have six dollars to my name; what will it be, Uber or meds? Only enough for one. Decisions, decisions," he said with a bitter smile.

After a while Jerry noticed the growing crowd outside, jumped off the bed with child-like energy and put on his best smile to go greet them. "There are my peeps!" he said as he opened his arms and began to embrace them, almost like they were that child he didn't have the chance to make amends with.

Some of the patients had colored pictures for him, others had written him goodbye letters and a few poems. They had also brought him gifts--menial knick-knacks, like hair combs, Bibles and used notebooks. Jerry knew that to some of them these were valuable possessions, and he showed sincere gratitude with smiles and hugs.

A well-groomed, older gentleman came up as Jerry still said his goodbyes.

"Jerry..." he said in a soft yet stern voice.

"Bob, glad you came by," Jerry said. "Let me introduce you to him."

They walked into the room and headed toward my bed, where I still lay, absorbing everything that was happening outside.

"Jay, this is Bob," Jerry said as I sat up. "He is a friend who has been having some issues with his roommate and I figured you two could bunk together."

"The son of a bitch wouldn't let me sleep with his babbling," Bob said as he extended his hand to shake mine.

"Jay doesn't snore or talk," Jerry intervened, "although he did scream somewhat loudly last night." He smiled.

"I thought you hadn't heard that!" I said, surprised.

"I hear everything," he smirked with a sense of pride.

A couple of hours later, Bob started to move his things into the room as Jerry prepared to make his way out. Meanwhile, I headed over to the nurse's station and politely asked the one by the computer if I could be escorted to the lockers to get something out.

She took me all the way to the back of the station to a small locker room, looked at the bracelet on my wrist and found the right locker, opening it with a three-digit combo. She then stood by my side as I dug in the bag to find my wallet, and inside a ten-dollar bill, the only one that had survived the madness of the previous weeks. It was all the money I had left in the world, and it would now help Jerry get his meds as well as a ride to nowhere, to face a bleak and uncertain future at best.

I stood by the counter at the nurse's station as the double doors swung open and Jerry went back to his reality. As I saw him walk out, I couldn't believe that in such a short amount of time this man had grown so much on me. But he had, and I knew that in the limited moments we shared, we both had a positive impact on each other's lives. I was extremely grateful for that.

Thank you for your service to our country, Jerry. Your courage, honor and sacrifice should not be forgotten.

Hurrah.

Will the medication transform you into the version of yourself that is acceptable to society?

CHAPTER 8

One o'clock was mid-afternoon medication time, and a small line of anxious patients was already growing in front of the pharmacy door. "Meds, come get your meds, please!" A couple of nurses knocked on all the bedroom doors to ensure everyone else came out and took their pills. Many patients loved their drugs; they yearned for them. The addicts were the first ones in line to receive their dosages of Xanax, Klonopin or Valium. Even if they were tapered dosages, something was better than nothing.

Other patients, however, did not share the same enthusiasm. The paranoid ones were difficult to convince to ingest any type of substance, especially in pill form. They saw drugs as a tool for mind control, maybe even a government conspiracy that would allow those of higher rank total ability to monitor, adjust and implant their thoughts. It wasn't unusual to see a nurse showing a pill wrapper to wary patients who wanted to make sure they knew what they were taking. Even then, they would not be satisfied, and it sometimes took special "persuasion" tactics in order to medicate them.

Tara had the odd suspicion that the pharmacy lady had it in for her and insisted in seeing the imprints on every pill, plus a document that showed what those markings meant. The nurse would have to go on Wikipedia and print out a copy of the medication page that usually contained a picture of the pill, so Tara could compare. Sometimes, if the pill looked different on the printout (pills are manufactured by different companies and different dosages of the same drug don't look the same) it was nearly impossible to convince her to take it. She would clench her teeth and lock her mouth shut, and no one could talk her into changing her mind. She had visible bruises on her arms where shots had to be administered because of her refusal to cooperate. "They have no compassion," she would say. "How can they be doctors and nurses when they treat the sick without compassion?"

I stood in line to get my first dosage of the meds that Dr. Patel had prescribed. I hoped that it would somehow help me alleviate the indescribable amount of pain that I carried. It was a similar pain that had previously made me the worst pharmacist in the world, "prescribing" myself a ridiculous amount of anti-anxiety pills that didn't kill me because it was difficult and expensive to get more consistently, and that put me in such a downward spiral that deploying a parachute out of my back would not have slowed me down enough to make a difference. Still, standing there, in the pharmacy line, the hairs in the back of my head stood, thinking about the possibility of the pharmacist (overwhelmed by all the patients and trying to keep track of everything) royally screwing up and giving me someone's dose of benzos by mistake. A couple of milligrams of Xanax, man, that would put me in the perfect place... no, no... I should stash them, and wait until the evening to get more, yes... and then crush them into a fine powder, mix it in a cup of coffee and head down to the TV room to watch the NBA finals. Curry vs Lebron. It was going to be a good series, and an even better one with a decent buzz.

Ladies and Gentlemen, the mind of an addict hard at work.

The odds of that happening, however, were zero to none. The pharmacy had a pill machine that dispensed the medication after the patient's bracelet had been scanned, matching them up with the doctor's prescription on file. There could not be any foul play, but an addict could always dream.

I quietly stood in line as several screams broke behind me, the terrified hollers of patients who thought they were being killed with a shot. I reached the pharmacy door, which was split in the middle so the top part could be opened while the bottom one stayed closed, serving as a counter. The nurse behind it asked for my hand and scanned the bracelet. The machine started making a mechanical sound that made me wonder if it was fabricating the pills right there and then. After two or three seconds, it spat out one tablet, which the nurse took out of the wrapper with urgency, put in a small cup and gave to me, along with some water.

"Effexor, 75mg. Drink please. Swallow. Open your mouth for me, stick out your tongue. Let me see under. Good. Thank you. Next!"

I walked across the hall, all the way to the end of the floor, where there was a glass window that spanned the entire height of the wall. Through it you could see across the city: the towering skyscrapers of the downtown skyline that flirted with the curious clouds, the water tower that had just been repainted after getting vandalized by "artists," the freeway that would always get congested during rush-hour traffic, and the little coffee shop that we would frequent, where the lattes were handcrafted to perfection and the stories we told, for some reason, tasted better. In the distance, you could hear cars zooming by, going only-God-knew where in the middle of the day. The medical offices below had people going in and out of them consistently, completely oblivious of what was going on in the world around them, especially up here. From this high up they looked insignificant, like faceless dummies that were put in place to simply be part of the landscape. Where they were headed and why, what they were thinking that kept them up at night, what motivated them to get out of bed in the morning, what lies they told others and even themselves, who made them smile, who made them cry, or cringe with anger, what made them dream and what made them scared... it didn't matter. They didn't matter, and we didn't matter to them.

I rested my forehead on the glass and felt the heat of a sun that had already been knocking on it for a few hours. It was a big difference from the frigidity of the temperature on this side of the window. I closed my eyes and stood there for a few seconds, wishing the heat in my forehead would travel through the rest of my body, wanting the window to disappear and for the sun to shine directly on my face. Behind me the noises began to dissipate, the meds started to kick in and most patients retracted to their rooms for their mid-afternoon, drug-induced naps.

A compact car drove into the parking lot and did a couple of rounds, trying to find an empty space. It was a familiar make and model, which slightly caught my attention. An SUV left and freed up a spot, which the small car quickly took advantage of. The driver-side door swung open, and out of it walked a woman, well dressed, high heels, long hair. I could not distinctly make out her face, but I knew it was her. My stomach jumped with both enthusiasm and fear. *Did she hear that I was here? Did she come to see me and check in on me?* A thousand thoughts were going through my head as my heart rate accelerated and I began to tremble with nervousness. I followed her with my eyes as she walked toward one of the doors below when, halfway there, she stopped and began searching for something in her purse. When she could not find it, she turned around and began trotting back toward the car, carefully, trying not to take a misstep on high heels. That's when I was able to see the outline of her face, instantly realizing that it wasn't the woman I thought it was. I took a second look and understood it had all been a delusion; I wasn't even familiar with a car that make and color.

Feeling disappointed and defeated, I remained standing by the window, forehead on the glass, questioning whether I was going to make it out of this place alive, or at least somewhat sane.

I felt it in the middle of my stomach first, a gentle euphoria rapidly growing inside me and making its way toward my brain. My hands got tingly, and then my head. My ears started to buzz a little. My heart beat accelerated and I felt as if I could succeed at taking over the world, and I wanted to. It was a dramatic change from the way I had been feeling a few seconds before. I couldn't quite explain it, but I was happy. As a norepinephrine reuptake inhibitor, Effexor, among other things, blocks the reabsorption of adrenaline in the brain, leading to an energetic and sometimes slightly euphoric state. This side effect, of course, would diminish after a few days, but for now it was definitely a big change in the way I had been feeling. *I'll take it!* I said to myself. If I felt like this all the time, the sky was the limit on all the things I could accomplish.

For a minute, I didn't know whether to do jumping jacks or slide across the floor in my socks, to see how fast I could make it to the other side. I decided against that, however, as I thought the nurses would probably not appreciate it. Instead I chose to put my newfound energy to good use and take a shower. I picked up a towel, a small bottle of shampoo and some liquid soap at the front desk and jumped in the cold but soothing waters of the public shower. There was no lock on the door and, concerned with the risk of someone forgetting to knock (which I'm sure happened often), I took care of business quickly and got out feeling lighter, not only because I had washed some of the dirt away, but also because the weight I was carrying on my shoulders significantly diminished.

CHAPTER 9

I sat in the lounge area, forced to wear a green hospital gown, not having a clean change of clothes after the shower. I sat in dreadful solitude until I could sit no more, the broken clock laughing at my lack of patience. I then got up and completed a few laps of the almost empty floor, checked out the TV room for a while and finally decided to head back to my room, to once again stare at the stars through the ceiling. As I walked in, I noticed Bob lying in his bed, glasses halfway down his nose, reading his Bible out loud.

"Why died I not from the womb? – It would surely have been far better, and much happier for me, had I either expired in the womb where I received my life, or had it been taken from me the very moment my eyes saw the light of this world..."

"Job was a troubled man," Bob said as he turned the page.

"Everything that meant anything had been abruptly taken from him by the only God he knew." He took his eyes of the Bible and made eye contact with me. "Are you a God-fearing man, Jay?"

"I have always feared God... Loved, on the other hand..." I replied.

Bob smiled and turned his eyes back to the written word. "If I was to guess I would say that many people here feel like Job did, demolished and desolated, regretting their own births, having lost their path in life."

"I guess that's a fair assumption," I said, hoping that the conversation would not turn into a sermon.

He began turning pages until he reached his desired text. *"Finally, Job died, after a long and satisfying life."* He smiled again, his face reflecting assertion. "It's difficult to understand how after all he went through he still lived a full and satisfying life, but you see, Jay," he took his glasses off, "God never left his side, not even once, even when Job thought he was alone, regretting his own existence. God was there, God remembered. I have the feeling God is here as well."

"I hope you are right, Bob," I said, trying not to sound sarcastic. I had always been strongly encouraged, sometimes even forced, to love God and be close to him, but after so many trials and tribulations, I grew convinced that God just didn't care, especially about me. I was hesitant to think that this place would change my mind, or that God would try to somehow reconnect with me here.

"I know so!" Bob said with tremendous conviction.

He was a man past his prime, but well conserved and with a great sense of style. He wore well-ironed shirts and slacks that were clearly brand name clothing. It was hard to grasp how someone could manage to look so impeccable in this place, but he did. His tone was always soft but direct. His demeanor inspired respect, but not fear. He was the kind of man you could rely on for sincere advice, a straight shooter who would tell it like it was without hindering your self-worth in the process.

What the hell is he doing in here? I could not help but wonder. I thought about asking him, but I didn't want to come off nosey. After all we had just met and were going to be roommates for probably the next few days. I didn't want to make an awkward move that I would later regret.

He got out of the bed, put on a pair of leather flip flops and straightened out the sheets. He put the Bible under his arm and looked at me. "I'm going to go for a snack; you coming?" I agreed without hesitation; the way he said it made it clear that he wasn't really asking.

The nurses would bring in a snack cart around three-thirty in the afternoon, when the meds would start wearing off and half-awake patients would start crawling out of their rooms. There were generic chocolate chip cookies, boxed milk, tiny cereal boxes and a nice assortment of candies. Bob and I sat in front of the broken clock as he sipped on multi-color cereal and I made funny faces, munching on Sour Patch Kids.

"My wife, Olivia, doesn't allow me to have much sugar," Bob grinned as he slurped on the now pinkish blue milk. "This place has its benefits, you see."

"You are a glass half full kind of guy, I take it," I said, in the midst of battling the Sour Patch Kid in my mouth.

"When you end up here at my age, you *have* to have a sense of humor, my friend." There was barely any cereal left in the bowl and Bob now lifted the whole thing toward his mouth to finish the rest of the milk.

"I'm going to be honest with you, Bob, you don't seem like the rest of them here," I mentioned.

"Neither do you," Bob replied, without taking the bowl away from his face. He finished what was left of the milk and looked at the inside of the bowl, almost as if he was trying to find the story of his own life somewhere in there.

"I spent twenty-five years doing my part in keeping the streets of Cincinnati clean, and handing out a few speeding tickets here and there. Being a police officer is challenging work, but I enjoyed it and did well. Before that I defended our freedom across the world, in places I reckon should not exist. God was always with me, protecting me and reminding me of my purpose. Even in the darkest days I felt his presence; he never left my side, and I thank him for that. Little did I know that the battlefield would not be where I would fight the toughest war. After retirement, I still felt like I had something left to give, and when my younger brother asked me to come down to Florida and help him with his property business, I made him believe it was a tough decision, but it wasn't," he laughed. "Trading snow for sunshine was a no-brainer, and Olivia and the girls had family here so they were thrilled.

"Nine months later I was on the floor with serious back injury after the ladder I was on gave out underneath me. Surgery didn't help much, if at all, and I spent the following year surviving on opioid patches and pain-killer cocktails. I have never been much of a drinker myself, so I never thought these prescriptions would bring me to my knees like they did.

"But bring me to my knees they did, and here I am, finishing the last leg of my detox. After a severe stint with depression and an almost successful suicide attempt, I decided Olivia and the girls deserved better." He opened a second box of milk and began pouring its contents into the bowl. Then came more cereal. "How about you-- what brings you to this neck of the woods?"

"Well, my story is a little longer," I replied, "with some of the same characters in play, I'm afraid, except the ladder and the bad back. For me the depression came with the package."

"When did you realize that you were depressed?" Bob asked.

"Fifteen years too late, after way too many alcohol binges, blacked-out nights and damaged lives. But I guess it started when I was nine."

"Nine..." Bob said softly, doing calculations in his head. "That's a long time, my friend, I don't know if I would have been able to endure for that long."

"Neither do I," I replied. "Hence the reason for being unconscious half the time."

Bob lowered his head in thought momentarily, then raised his eyes and looked at me, while manufacturing a comforting grin.

"Yet here we are…"

"Yet here we are…" I reciprocated the smile.

"Well, visitation is in a few hours. I should go freshen up for my girls," he said as he set aside the plastic bowl and stood up from his chair. "I enjoyed the talk, Jay; let's do it again."

It didn't take me long after he walked away to realize that he had left his Bible behind. It was still open to the book of Job. I reached across the table and pulled it to my side.

Job 1:8 – And The Lord said unto Satan: Have you considered my servant Job, that there is no one like him in the earth, a perfect and upright man, one that feared God, and eschewed evil?

Damn, I thought. Why would God point Job out like that, and to Satan no less! Threw him right under the bus.

Best to stay off God's radar, I guess.

CHAPTER 10

Meatloaf, corn, mashed potatoes and biscuits were served for dinner, and everyone seemed quite excited about such a fancy meal. Dinner usually consisted of stale hamburger patties and a handful of cold vegetables. The cart would be rolled in around five to six, and nurses would start pulling out the trays at six on the dot. All of them were labeled with the patients' names to make sure that those with dietary restrictions received the appropriate meal, which had been put together in the kitchen according to doctor's instructions.

The lounge would gradually transform into the dining area and tables would fill up with patients who, much like in high school, knew where to sit and who to sit with. Being the new kid on the block meant that I would still have to sit alone, unless Bob did me a solid and joined me. But he didn't; he must have been too full on breakfast cereal and not on the Holy Word, as he took two quick bites of his food and retreated to the room to read some more.

The zombies usually gathered toward the back of the lounge, eating barely enough for sustenance, and doing it at a dreadful pace. The homeless were always close to the food cart, waiting for any opportunity to grab seconds or leftovers. After they were done with their food they would usually start scavenging other tables, asking people for what they didn't want. The lucid took ownership of the front tables and talked sports, tried to flirt with the pretty nurses, told dirty jokes and traded food items for cigarettes.

Donna the diabetic had to be carefully monitored, as she would try to sneak extra biscuits into her gown and save them for a midnight snack, literally risking her life. The blind man didn't want to eat, and continued clenching his teeth every time the spoon got close to his mouth. The nurse who was trying to feed him held it there for a few seconds and, when his hand got too tired to hold it up, he set it back on the tray, threw it in the trash and went behind the desk to resume his clerical work on the keyboard, without the slightest concern whether the blind man lived or died from starvation. Tara walked around with urgency, making sure that no one's meatloaf had boogers in it. "Sit down, relax and eat, Tara!" one of the nurses yelled out, but Tara ignored the call and continued pacing nervously from table to table, closely studying everyone's food, much to the annoyance of those sitting at them.

The whole scene felt like being part of the most dysfunctional family ever during Thanksgiving dinner. It was a collage of multicolored imperfections, an internal combustion engine whose timing was extremely off. But it kept ticking, and somehow, it worked just well enough for it not to be exceedingly unpleasant.

I sat alone at the table, attempting to swallow the meatloaf whole, when a small shadow covered part of the tray and went up toward my face.

"There he is! My savior!" Tara announced. "How's your meatloaf, any boogers?"

"No, no boogers here Tara," I replied, forcing a smile.

"Good, I'm glad," she said. "Last time they had meatloaf they were full of boogers and maggots and little spiders that would crawl up your nostrils and infect your brain. A few guys here had brain infections for a while…"

My lower jaw dropped and let a piece of half chewed meatloaf fall to the plate.

"I actually wrote a note to the director, you know," she continued, "to tell him about the maggots and the shots and the way nurses handle things around here, which is inhumane! And I... I handed it to him and said: *Director, this is secret information that you need to know*, and he said: *Tara, you have done a good job!* And that's how he..." she lowered her voice and reached across the table to get closer to me, "...shhhhhh... don't tell anyone," she whispered. "That's how I became a secret spy for the director..."

I lazily nodded with eyes wide. "Very interesting, good job, Tara," I said, trying to sound genuinely impressed.

She stood there for what seemed to be an eternity and looked at me. Her pupils dilated and her cheeks got rosy red.

"You're sexy..." she whispered, still loud enough that everyone heard what she said. Silence covered the entire lounge, and curious looks were thrown my way.

I was at a loss for words. "Tha... thank you," I uttered, trying to hide my disbelief at what I was experiencing.

She looked at me for a few more moments, quietly. Then her wheels began spinning again and she moved on to the next table, where she wasn't greeted with the same enthusiasm.

"Tara, stop your nonsense and just sit down and eat!"

"Fine, eat boogers then!" Tara yelled back as she walked harshly across the lounge to sit and eat her food. She looked like a child who had been scolded and forced to sit down to finish her meal. She took one bite of her meatloaf, spat it back out and slapped the entire tray off the table with unusual strength. "Great! Roaches this time!" she screamed as she ran toward her room and a nurse chased after her.

The engine continued to struggle and misfire, but it did not cease. Everyone ate, and when it was over, they all dispersed, some to the solitude of their rooms, others to watch TV, and a few to the small gated courtyard to smoke. I opted for lying on the bed and listening to an inspired Bob read some of his favorite Bible passages out loud. It was the closest thing that I had to music, and his voice, although passionate, was also remarkably soothing.

Thanksgiving dinner on a summer night, with the most dysfunctional family in the world. Not as bad as I thought it would be. The meatloaf could have used some help, though.

CHAPTER 11

Visitation started at seven-thirty, after the trays were gone and the dining area was again the lounge. Visitors would get badges with their pictures on them, get clearance to walk in through the double doors, and for up to an hour, they were able to join their loved ones in the colorful madness that was the psychiatric floor.

Bob was the first one to receive family, and he now sat in front of the nurse's station with two grown women on his lap. His girls were not really *girls* anymore, but beautiful elegant blondes who looked like twins, but weren't. His wife was also beautiful, and she stood next to them with arms crossed, doing the best she could not to laugh at Bob's shenanigans, but miserably failing. It was easy to see that Bob felt at home wherever his family was; it was all he needed to be happy, to feel alive. As long as there were three smiling women somewhere in his vicinity, he was the most fortunate man in the world.

Donna the diabetic received her oldest son, who seemed to be lecturing her on how she needed to take better care of herself. I guess he had gotten the memo from the nurses on the illegal biscuit operation. I was too far to hear what he was saying, but I could tell he was speaking lovingly, yet with a strong tone of voice. She wasn't paying any attention to what he said though; she just smiled and kept her hand on his cheek, as if nothing else in the world mattered but that cheek.

Big Mike's girlfriend showed up rather briefly, and with a swift move slapped Mike in the face and walked right out. "Damn, I guess I forgot to lock my phone!" he laughed, as if this wasn't the first time it happened, and it wouldn't be the last.

There was an elderly woman who sat alone in the back of the lounge, close to the broken clock. She was short in stature and sweet in the eyes, bathed in the curls of her silver hair. She broke down in tears as soon as she laid eyes on the hunched old man who walked through the doors. He pushed his tired feet to get to her as fast as they could, and they then held each other as he joined her in weeping, instantly creating an intimate moment of love, difficult to forget. But her recent diagnosis said otherwise, and she wanted to keep him close to her for as long as the memories were there, for as long as they meant something. Decades of stories they had written together, of trips to far parts of the world, of babies who grew up too soon, of grandchildren who loved them too much, of slow dances in the evenings while listening to old records, and warm embraces in the cool nights of winter, when the heater didn't work right, and all they needed was each other--their withered bodies, which had fused together a long time ago, doing the job that no heater could… all that and more, gone, effortlessly, the flaw of a mind that refused to hold on. Sometimes there is nothing crueler than life itself, which gives us so much, then takes pleasure in taking it away.

Many patients sat in the lounge waiting for visitors who would never come. Some of them knew the bitter truth; others were totally unaware. They gleamed with hope every time the double doors swung open, not knowing all they had was inside these walls. They had been abandoned by a world in which they didn't fit, a world that rejected them. Family members reached breaking points; they didn't have the strength to bear it any longer, they didn't want to. They became part of a system good enough to keep them alive but not fix them, designed to modify them into medicated zombies who felt nothing, or at least couldn't show it. That way no one was bothered with guilt or remorse for them; no one felt motivated to love them.

I continued to helplessly absorb the panorama when I felt a hand rest on my shoulder. "How is it going kid?" Dad asked, holding back some tears.

"It's going," I replied, trying to hide my excitement at seeing them again. It had felt like years.

Mom came up behind him and clung to my neck for a while, letting the silence linger. Eventually they sat down in the chairs across the table, meticulously studying me, trying to deduce if I was doing any better.

"How are you feeling?" Mom asked, as Dad looked over his shoulder at the movement behind him, a little concerned. Coming from the outside world to an unpredictable environment that didn't click quite right could be a tad unnerving.

"Somewhat better. The medications help," I replied.

"Well, that's good to hear," Dad said. "That is the reason you are here, to get you feeling better. Did you sleep ok?"

"I guess, as good as you can sleep in here…"

"Did you see the doctor? What did they say?" Mom asked.

"Dr. Patel heard me out for a while and prescribed a couple of meds. She has some ideas, but nothing concrete yet. I guess we have to wait a little longer, until I get to talk more with her."

"Ok then…" Mom said, a little disappointed. "We will know soon; all that matters right now is that you are feeling better, and that you are safe."

"I gotta say," Dad smiled, trying to steer the conversation elsewhere, "green is definitely not your color." He was referring to the hideous hospital gown I had no choice but to wear.

"Yeah, I've noticed," I laughed. "Unfortunately, this is the only clean piece of clothing I have."

"Not true, not anymore!" Mom jumped in and handed me the bag she had by her legs. In it were two pairs of jeans, a few t-shirts, plenty of underwear for an extended stay and my favorite piece of clothing: my black jacket. It was a double-rider made with full grain leather, with beautiful top stitching and both body and sleeve linings. It had been my high school graduation gift and it had not been cheap. I felt like a bad-ass every time I wore it.

"One of the nurses already checked everything in before we came in, so please change out of that abomination as soon as we leave. I don't want you looking like the rest of *them*," she said in a hushed tone.

Mom had always been a fan of dressing me up. She would get mad when I stayed in my pajamas all day, on those lazy weekends that I had nothing to do but stay home. Sundays, especially, she would have an outfit picked out and ready, no matter if we were going anywhere or not. Grandma had been a seamstress most of her life, and she enjoyed making outfits for me when I was little, so Mom would usually put me on one of her creations on Sundays, and the habit stuck with me. No matter what, I always found myself looking for nicer attire in my closet on a Sunday morning. Sometimes, however, I would be so out of my mind intoxicated that I would pass out in front of the closet and not even get to put on any clothes. Sunday mornings were also my favorite hours to get messed up.

We got lost in conversation and talked about a bit of everything. Mom reminisced on the past and how hard it was to get me to shower when I was younger. Dad remembered the first time he had to spank me after I tried to cross the street by myself, and how much he secretly cried afterwards. I remembered the first time they took me to the circus, and how terrified I was of the elephants. We laughed out loud at things we hadn't thought about for years, like the fifteen-year-old girl I fell in love with when I was six, and the time I sat on my uncle's motorcycle and the whole thing fell on me, almost breaking my leg. We talked about those people who came and went, those moments engraved in our history, the times when we thought things were going great, but in retrospect, we were just lying to ourselves.

Before we knew it, the nurses were letting everyone know that visitation time was over. Mom somberly hung from my neck for a while again, and Dad gave me two soft pats on the shoulder as he walked away. I hadn't felt this close to them in years, and my heart felt like it was being squeezed as I watched them walk out the double doors.

"You are a fortunate man," a voice broke the silence out of nowhere. I turned around in the chair to notice an old, very wrinkled man sporting a wooden cane, standing a few feet behind me, in the shadow of the column next to the table. "I forgot what it was like…" he said in a broken voice as his eyes traveled to the past, and wondered, and reminisced.

"To have visitors?" I asked, intrigued.

"No," he replied, vaguely annoyed. He looked almost through me, his eyes scavenging my innermost spirit. "To have someone who cares." He stood in silence as he allowed me to digest his answer. He then calmly walked away as the cane made light thumps on the floor, and the old man disappeared in the darkness of the now dim-lit floor. It was interesting that I had never seen the old man before, and after that, I never saw him again.

I hadn't considered myself fortunate for a long time, maybe ever. But at that very moment I had an important epiphany: rock bottom was still a few levels down from where I was standing.

Who would've thought.

CHAPTER 12

The minimum therapeutic dose of Seroquel is 300mg. As an antipsychotic, it promotes clearer thoughts and can also help with depression and anxiety. One major side effect of the drug, however, is sleepiness, and for that reason Dr. Patel prescribed me 100mg before bed to help me rest, and to titrate the medicine in case I needed larger dosages later.

I took the pill at nine and decided to head to the TV room to check out the game for a bit. Big Mike and a few others were already there, locked into the right channel, ready to go. It was the NBA finals, Cavs vs. Warriors, LeBron vs. Curry. It had the making of a great series.

I became a fan of basketball in the nineties, the Jordan days. I recorded the entire 98 finals on my old VCR, when the Chicago Bulls defeated the Utah Jazz and Michael had one of the best performances of his career. I got so hooked on the game that I begged my dad to buy me a basketball hoop, and after pleading non-stop for a couple of weeks, he finally caved in. The driveway became my personal court, and I would be out there every day, all by myself, acting out entire series in my head. I played the role of both teams, the fans and the commentators, giving my best effort on each side, no matter who I pretended to be. I even had imaginary teammates who would perform based on the specific abilities I had given them. After every game, I recorded performance stats and standings, and eventually ended with playoff brackets. I never planned who would win; I would play it out, sometimes to my own disappointment. But the thrill of the game itself was all that mattered. Hearing the ball swoosh through the net gave me a certain sensation that was difficult to describe. I really enjoyed the game.

As the drinking began and the depression worsened, however, the enjoyment that I got out of basketball and other passions diminished, and the only thing that excited me anymore was the prospect of my next buzz. Basketball became a thing of the past, Jordan retired and the old VCR broke. I never recorded another game, and the basketball hoop on the driveway got rusty and lost the net.

I sat in the back of the TV room as Mike and his colleagues followed the play-by-play and offered their own commentary of the action. I did my best to focus and feel the same excitement for the game as I did before, but it didn't happen. It just wasn't the same. Disappointed with the numbness, I left the room shortly after and headed for the big window on the other side of the floor.

The view at night was different. The lights of the downtown skyline illuminated the sky for as far as my eye could see. In the distance, you could hear a few cars zooming quickly through the now almost empty freeway. An ambulance approached the hospital, its sirens screaming with desperation. Horns honked from time to time. A loud muffler begged for attention. A helicopter's flutter joined the colorful soundtrack of the night, as it landed with precision on the helipad. The parking lot below was now empty; the constant traffic of people had disappeared. The lights of the city dimmed the stars, and other than the moon and a lonely cloud, there was nothing else in the sky. The world, for some reason, felt bigger than usual, and I, smaller. I got a mental image of all the people who were maybe getting home - soaked in the stress of the day - kissing their significant others and throwing themselves on the couch, unwinding in front of the TV, working through a slice of cold pizza and perhaps a cup of wine within reach. I thought about those people who liked to go on jogs in the dark, attempting to sweat away their problems, or the ones who spontaneously decided to go for a fancy meal, without worrying about the amount of the check. I thought about those who were visiting loved ones, or painting, or listening to their favorite song, or playing their instrument of choice, or making passionate love, or living life on their own terms, proud of their accomplishments, satisfied with whatever footprint they would leave behind. I thought, and the more I thought, the smaller I felt.

"It's a nice view," a voice penetrated my right ear. I had been so focused on the other side of the window and so deep in thought that I failed to notice the woman standing next to me, with her head against the glass, looking out at nothing in particular, soaked in relentless sadness, locked in a prison of her own despair. She was the one from the emergency room and the Prada luggage.

"Sure is," I whispered, as the glare of the moon reflected on the glass. She was a tall woman of fair skin, gold hair and dim blue eyes, not young, but well preserved. She wore Hello Kitty pajama pants, a Grateful Dead t-shirt and a pair of Ugg booties. She didn't look like she was going through a mid-life crisis; instead, it seemed she had just refused to grow old, and the years reluctantly obliged.

"Not the city I expected to see out the window tonight, but it's a nice view, I'll admit," she said with disappointment.

"So your stay in this phenomenal facility was not part of the plan?" I asked, sarcastically.

"No, even though the accommodations here are first class, this was definitely NOT part of the plan," she said, accurately mirroring my sarcasm.

"Where then, where else but here would you rather be?" I inquired.

"Fort Lauderdale," she answered. "The New Beginnings Spa Resort."

"Rehab?" I asked.

She nodded.

"I have the feeling the accommodations there were much nicer," I said.

"Much nicer!" she smiled. "Luxury bedrooms, state of the art gym and sauna, gardens that would make Solomon envious, and the food, oh the food, definitely no boogers!"

We looked at each other and immediately erupted in uncoordinated laughter.

"There is also group therapy, meditation, personalized treatment and nursing staff that is very good at keeping drugs out of reach."

"I should keep one of those at home with me," I smirked.

"Yeah, if only," she chortled.

"Well, at least you did plenty of research on the place; you know it well."

"It would have been my fourth time there, so yeah, I know it very well." There was a sense of defeat in her voice.

"Ah, repeat customer, I see. I guess the place *is* nice," I said, hoping to bring her back to sarcastic instead of sad.

She kept looking out the window, but all I think she paid attention to was her own reflection on the glass. "The first few times it usually doesn't take, and, in all honesty, you usually don't care. You are there because someone made you and you have no choice. All you can think about is getting out and resuming the recklessness."

"And this time, you care?" I asked, genuinely interested in what she had to say.

"Well, yeah!" she laughed. "Daddy threatened to completely cut me off!"

Her sly smile dissipated and morphed into concern. "I'm too old for this shit, man. I need to get a grip one way or another, but these pills, they keep calling my name..."

"I feel you there." Her concern was now reflected on me, her regrets something I could relate with. "And speaking of names, yours?" I asked.

"Callie…" She stuck her hand straight out, almost like a low salute.

"Jay…" I shook it back, noticing that her grip was unusually strong.

"So enlighten me, Callie," I asked. "You are on your way to the New Beginnings Spa Resort, where the beds are fluffy and the meals are five-star quality… how do you deviate and end up here?"

"Where the beds are NOT so fluffy," she scoffed. "I actually made it to rehab, but being sober for longer than twenty-four hours brings out the not-so-pleasant version of Callie. Checking in, one of the nurses discovered the secret stash hidden in the luggage, and I get incredibly angry when someone touches my Blues. It's almost like a survival reflex."

"I see…"

"Long story short, I threatened to kill everyone who touched my shit and myself if they kept harassing me, so the cops were called and I was Baker Acted. That is how I ended up in this fine establishment."

"Well…" I said. "Look at it the good way. It's a beautiful night, and we have this nice view."

"It *is* a nice view," she smirked. "And the meatloaf wasn't half bad."

"You're right, it was terrible!" I yelled, making both of us erupt in laughter again.

Suddenly, I started feeling my eyelids get three times as heavy, so heavy it was challenging to keep them up. I had to focus much harder on my balance, as my knees became weak and the sound of Callie's voice became muffled and distant. "I… gotta go," I said. "Sleeping pill, kicking in."

"Ah, they got you on the good stuff, I see. Well, it was nice to meet you, Jay; catch you some other time!"

"Catch... some... othe... ti..." I mumbled as I waved my hand in the air and stumbled toward the room - which felt farther than ever before - where I luckily landed in my bed, just in time to take off my socks and pass out.

That night I didn't hear the air conditioning's banter, and I honestly couldn't tell if Bob snored or not. I never heard the nurse barging in every twenty minutes, or was bothered by the light hitting my face repeatedly. That morning, when the blood pressure machine stood bedside, all that came out from under the sheets was my arm, and when the procedure was over it retracted back to the warmth and I continued sleeping. No nightmares, no torture.

Pure, unadulterated sleep.

CHAPTER 13

There she was, angel bright and pearl white, glowing like the most beautifully dangerous and radioactive human being on the planet. She was wearing nothing but a see-through baby-doll that left just enough to the imagination. Her legs were longer than I could remember, her breasts were perkier, her body a commentary on the intricate details of womanly beauty. She was amazingly feminine and desirable and sexual. My heart pounced on my ribcage, like a madman forcefully shakes the jail bars in a deranged attempt at escaping.

She got on the bed and slowly crawled on her hands and knees toward me, biting her lower lip. Her waist waved from side to side with the fluidity of a big cat as it approaches its prey. Her long straight hair covered part of her face and caressed the sides of her breasts. She got close enough for me to feel her minty breath wrap around my lips. "Baby..." she whispered.

"You came back," I exclaimed in a ruptured voice filled with nostalgia and regret, as I extended my hand and gently caressed her cheek. She leaned on my hand, and I felt the weight of her tenderness on my palm. She closed her eyes and smiled. "I did. I'm here. Never leaving again, babe."

A lonesome tear ran down my face. I was engulfed with an overwhelming fear that was hard to contain, an anxiety that compelled me to lose sight of my senses, of my logic, my truth.

"Baby, please," I begged, "never leave me again; please babe, I will never again..."

"Shhhh," she put her index finger on my lips, her eyelids fell slightly, and her mouth softened with kindness. "Shhhh now."

She grabbed my wrists and pushed my hands back against the pillow, held them there, hopped on top of me and began sensually thrusting, fabricating an incredible amount of pleasure for the both of us.

She arched back as her breasts danced carelessly on my face. I could tell she focused on the lovemaking, on the pure enjoyment of two humans colliding in intense titillation, but my satisfaction came from just having her there, close to me. I freed my hands, grabbed her waist and kept her as close to me as I could, feeling every square inch of curvy real estate as it created intense friction against mine, every elevated hair, every sweaty pore, every perfectly placed freckle.

After several moments of profound ecstasy, I noticed that her body was gradually morphing into one I didn't know. Her hands became smaller and her fingers stubbier, her waist widened and her curves were now jagged. The timing of her movements changed; what was once pleasurable was now painful. Her performance began to lack charm and elegance; it felt juvenile and forced. Part of her skin began to break apart and pixelate, just like when an online video has a hard time buffering.

I gradually opened my eyes, still feeling the heaviness of the medication. After regaining focus, I went into defense mode and let out a loud "AHHH," sitting up on the bed and throwing the naked woman who was on top of me to the floor.

There was a loud thump as Tara's body hit the floor, and another when her head hit the wall. She lay motionless for a few seconds, her brain trying to process the situation. When she realized what had occurred, the floodgates of tears opened and she ran out of the room crying, naked, holding her clothes in her hand.

It took me some time to make sense of everything that just happened, starting with the dream that, for obvious reasons, was extremely vivid. Then I struggled to figure out how to feel about the whole thing. Violated? Flattered? Both? Should I tell the nursing staff? How much trouble would Tara get in? Should I go talk to her? What should I say? I needed advice, and I knew the one person in the joint who could give it well.

Bob was sitting in the lounge, reading his Bible, waiting for the breakfast cart to show up. There were a few patients meandering; the rest were still in their rooms enjoying a last few drug-addled snoozes. His lips moved as he read and his glasses hung halfway down his nose, eyes strained in intense focus. "I need help," I said in a frantic tone, as I sat down on the chair across from him.

"We all do." He flipped the page and continued reading, as if what I'd said was an afterthought.

"I woke up to Tara sitting on me, naked." Now his lips stopped, his eyes moved away from the Bible and he looked at me over the glasses. I had his attention.

"Go on..." he uttered.

"She was, you know, um, naked, and she, was thrusting, back and forth, on top of me." I could feel the embarrassment crawling through my skin.

"What did you do?" he asked, intrigued.

"Well, when I opened my eyes and saw her I was shocked, so I instinctively pushed her off me. She fell and hit her head pretty hard, then ran out of the room crying. Naked."

Bob had been staring at me with a stern look the whole time, attempting to take what I was saying seriously, but couldn't hold the façade any longer. He exhaled in laughter, as if he was trying to cough out a piece of bagel that was stuck in his throat. "I gotta tell you, Jay," he yelled, "I'm glad I got up early today to give you guys your privacy!"

"OK, ok. Funny," I snarled, annoyed. "I need your advice. I don't know how to handle this whole mess."

He instantly morphed back into straight-shooter Bob, the Bob I had come to see. "The girl is quirky; she's got some issues for sure, but I don't think she means any harm."

"Should I tell the staff?"

"I don't think that would help. She would get scolded and probably lose some privileges, which I think would driver her crazier. I think you should go to her and talk it out, set some boundaries."

"You think she would understand, that she would comply?" I asked.

"I think she deserves a chance," Bob replied.

"I don't know, Bob, it's the second time I woke up and this girl was in the room. I don't know what she is capable of. Jerry even warned me about her. I'm seriously worried that I will wake up tomorrow and she will be slicing my throat with a plastic knife, or sucking the life out of me, like on those vampire flicks, or finally succeeding at taking advantage of me."

Bob grinned, closed his Bible and put both hands on top of it. He looked at me with familiar eyes. I had seen them when my father taught me important lessons, the ones you can only learn by living. I remember them well, those eyes, because they told me that my father loved me, and they told my father that the things he had gone through had not been in vain. "Close your eyes," Bob asked. I was hesitant at first, since closing your eyes in this place was inherently risky, but I knew he wanted to make a point, so I obliged. I then sat in darkness for several seconds, waiting for instructions.

"Now open them and look around you. What do you see?" he inquired.

The wheels of the breakfast cart could be heard in the distance as it made its way past the double doors. Two nurses ran around knocking and yelling on every room, and groggy faces began to appear, taking their usual place in the lounge of the psychiatric floor. Donna the diabetic already stood in line before the cart was even in position. She wanted to make sure to get dibs on her cherished, potentially lethal biscuits. As she stood there, she held up her right arm with a smile, cupping and caressing an invisible cheek. She was filled with contentment, stroking the emptiness that her mind transformed into a loving son. Donnie sat at the table across from Big Mike, slurring some sort of hypothesis a hundred miles per hour, doing his abnormal gestures and drawing a strange symbol on the corner of an old newspaper. Mike just sat there fluffing his afro with a comb, indulging Donnie by nodding and smiling from time to time, even though he didn't comprehend a word he said. They were an eclectic duo to say the least, but for some reason they felt attracted to each other. The crooked eye lady dragged her feet through the hall, today at an unusual pace. She smiled and talked to the friends that she (and the meds) had been able to make. It was comforting not to see her in agony for once. I wondered how long it would last until she had to unwillingly return to her usual anguish. Oliver sat in his wheelchair in front of the nurse's station, seeing the light of his past through the infinite darkness in his eyes. Sometimes I wondered if he preferred being blind, to avoid seeing the true darkness that surrounded him. Maggie, who didn't talk, sat reclusively at the table at the end, where she knew no one else would join her. She never socialized with anyone, but that morning, when the lounge came alive with the buzz of patients, I saw a little spark in her eyes. She felt comfort being surrounded by others, and her face slightly (but surely) showed it. Tara came out momentarily, but as soon as she got sight of me her face crumpled up, she began to sob and quickly rushed back to the safety of her room.

I saw the floor gradually fill up with souls of remarkable disadvantage. I saw pain, I saw suffering, I saw pity and cruelty and loss. I saw innocence and ignorance, fear and love. I saw many things that moment, but none of those things were hope.

As I continued to helplessly absorb all that surrounded me, I began to realize that I wasn't just observing the landscape; I was very much a part of it. It was then when Bob opened the Bible and began to read aloud a passage from Matthew. *"He went through all the towns and villages, teaching in their synagogues, proclaiming the good news of the kingdom and healing every disease and sickness. When he saw the crowds, he had compassion on them, because they were harassed and helpless, like sheep without a shepherd."*

My eyes welled up and a few tears painted lines on my face, this time not because I was feeling the sting of depression, or loneliness or fear, not because I was drowning in a sea of self-pity, thinking I was less than nothing. This time I cried because I saw the futility of lives that did not get a choice, of souls that were chained to their destiny with unbreakable links, of people who would never see the colors they deserved to see, who would never feel the love they deserved to feel, or live the lives they deserved to live. I saw them, and in them I saw me.

"Talk to her," Bob said. "She deserves a chance."

Fear.

CHAPTER 14

"I was fifteen when I had my first alcoholic drink. My girlfriend's sister was a fan of sangria, and by the time we arrived at her house that Sunday afternoon, she already had a couple of pitchers ready, begging to be consumed.

"My girlfriend Natalie grew up in a Latin family that did not abide by the standard of the American drinking age. When she was a baby, her dad would dip her pacifier in his beer so she could get accustomed to the taste, and when her teeth started coming in they would rub her gums with rum, as anesthetic to numb the pain. I grew up in a Latin family where the head of the household (my grandfather) was a functioning alcoholic, and after he died of a heart attack at the premature age of forty-eight, there was never much alcohol in the house. Sometimes when we went out to dinner my dad would have one or two beers, but that was the extent of my early run-ins with alcohol.

"That afternoon the older sister greeted us at the door with two cups full of the stuff, doing a little dance that told us she had already been drinking some. She was a very well-known party girl, famous for throwing the most outrageous high school parties when the parents were out of town. She settled down some after she got married and had a kid, but every once in a while she would send the husband away to his parents with the baby, and have a "well-deserved chill weekend," where the sangria would flow from the heavens and her cup would never empty. This was one of those weekends, and for whatever reason, the loneliness had gotten to her (all her friends were somewhere else working hard at being adults), so she asked Natalie to come spend time with her. She now stood at the door with a sly smile, extending her arm, offering me a cup filled to the top with some of the sweet stuff. I was initially wary of partaking, but when you have a girlfriend for the first time in your life and she is already out-drinking you, it just isn't a good look.

"We walked to a backyard that accommodated a beautiful flower garden with an array of colorful roses, gardenias, lilies, daffodils and jasmines. The garden was landscaped to perfection, the grass vibrant green and evenly cut without blemishes. The flowers looked as if they were raised by hand, all the same height, all arranged in immaculate patches that in unison created a plethora of color, a feast for the eyes of anyone who loved nature, and even those who were indifferent to it. There was a white wooden gazebo in the center, strategically positioned to take advantage of the last sunrays of the afternoon, where one could just relax and leave behind the stresses of the day. Natalie's sister and her husband had dished out an inordinate amount of money to build the backyard that way, after the husband (an air traffic controller) had a major panic episode and the doctor recommended either that or an aquarium, and they never liked fish. Inside the gazebo was a couch swing, and the three of us pushed gently with our feet until we got a pleasant back-and-forth going. It was a September afternoon that announced the beginning of Fall. The air cut through our skin, refreshing and crisp, as we gently rocked, and if I lifted my feet through the motion I felt like I was flying. It was a very simple, yet quite liberating experience.

"I put the cup of sangria to my mouth and quickly chugged about half of it, to the dismay of Natalie and her sister. *I didn't know you were only supposed to sip on the stuff,* I explained. I thought it was just like drinking orange or lemon juice; the faster you drink it the more refreshing it feels. I was forced to admit, with a bit of embarrassment, that I had never had an alcoholic beverage before.

"After a few discreet chuckles and a thorough explanation on the appropriate drinking etiquette, I sat there with a half-full (or half empty, depending on your philosophical bend) cup of sangria in my hand, enjoying the hypnotizing breeze that was rare to experience this far south. The minutes passed and I forgot about the brand-new substance that was now being digested in my stomach, processed by my liver and lifted to my brain in my blood. As time continued its course, the world gradually slowed down and the landscape began to feel farther than it was. A slight and gentle euphoria crawled up my spine and caressed the side of my head. My legs and hands started feeling lighter; the air felt even more revitalizing. The colors of the landscape looked more vibrant and the flowers seemed like they reflected light.

"I felt a peace I had never felt before, a peace that took away every fear, every anxious thought. I found myself smiling without reason, consumed in thoughts I couldn't completely grasp, lost in a significant and powerful moment, impossible to ignore. I was experiencing a new reality; I saw things through the lens of new eyes. I felt embraced by my surroundings; the flowers danced together to the rhythm of the wind, the colors merged with life and created something unique, something that could not be explained; it could only be felt. I felt happy to be alive, privileged even. I thought about everything that consisted of being human, of understanding everything like we do, of seeing the world and molding it to our convenience, like no other life form can do. *What an incredible perspective*, I thought, *what an amazing gift*. My vision became narrow and focused; I wasn't hurting about the past or worried about the future. All I saw was what I had in front of me, the moment when time stood still, and I finally saw the world I always wanted to see. Why hadn't I been able to previously feel this bliss?

"A few years before he passed, my grandfather came home from work bathed in his usual stupor. His weekday routine consisted of working at the manufacturing plant until five o'clock, then swinging by the bar down the street and starting his drinking shift. By the time he got home (if he didn't black out at the bar), he was conscious enough to have a glass of milk, take off his socks and pass out on the couch. Mom was the only one who could convince him, in his inebriated state, to get up and go lie down on his bed, and she would have to physically support him as he stumbled on the way there.

"That night, for reasons unknown to me, Mom wasn't in the mood to deal with the situation, and when he showed up drunker than usual, she couldn't hide her anger or hold back her words. 'Why, Dad? Why do you do this to yourself? To us?!'

"Even though his lids were halfway down his lost eyes and his balance was the one of a boat on choppy seas, he was coherent enough to comprehend the question and come up with an honest answer. He was always an honest man, drunk or not, and that's what people appreciated most about him.

"'Fear...' he uttered, before he almost completely lost his balance and Mom had to dig her head under his armpit and guide him to bed once again.

"When I accidentally overheard Dad recounting that night years later, Grandpa's response always intrigued me. But that Sunday afternoon gifted me with the answer that previously eluded me, and I immediately knew that, for good or bad, alcohol would play a crucial role in my life.

"A couple of months later, when Natalie picked up the phone and was brave enough to admit that she had been spending time with someone else, and that she didn't want to see me again, I recalled the numbing characteristics of alcohol, and, having nothing to lose, reached out to it for support. My parents had hosted a small dinner for some friends the night before, and there were three beers left in the fridge, since no one in the group drank much. I ignored the protocol I had previously learned and chugged one beer after the other as fast as I could, focused solely on drowning the ineffable pain.

"What happened next, I can only remember in broken sections, as if someone had spliced my memory with scissors. I remember stealing Mom's keys and driving like a maniac to Natalie's house. I think I made it to the door and I might have knocked on it harder than a SWAT team on a sting operation, but no one seemed to have answered. Then I was yelling at her window, then her mom came outside and was yelling at me. I think I spat on her face but I'm not too sure. Then I was behind the wheel again, screaming at the top of my lungs, and then... black. Then a headache from hell and the light of morning slapping me across the face. Mom's car was wrecked in the front, wet dirt and grass all over it. Up to this day I do not remember how it happened, but needless to say, they were not at all thrilled, and the punishment was severe.

"A couple of years later, after I graduated, I started working at a small electronic shop, doing basic customer service and entering orders in the computer system. My dad knew one of the guys who managed the place, and as a favor to him, they hired me. I made minimum wage doing menial work, but I didn't mind it. I wasn't ambitious back then. Billy and KJ worked in the warehouse doing fulfillment, and although they were close to me in age, they already had plenty of connections in the alcohol sourcing department, so we instantly became close friends.

"Soon my weekends consisted of riding in the back of KJ's beat-up Integra, hitting up a couple of 'spots' and heading over to Billy's uncle's house (who was usually out of town on business) to get a decent buzz without anyone to bother us. We would sit on the couch with a bag of Doritos or maybe some Taco Bell (if we were feeling fancy) and drink away the afternoon while watching basketball games or movies on the TV. Sometimes I didn't even remember getting home; I would just wake up in my bed, tortured by a headache that became worse as my parents took turns in yelling at me.

"I never felt more alive than when I was sitting in the backseat of that car, windows down, a 32-ounce of Colt 45 or Old English between my legs. I held the entire world in the palm of my hand, and I had the power to do with it whatever I wanted to. Wind on my face, freedom on my lap, people to share the experience with. It felt to me at the time that no other experience could rival that. I wanted to somehow find a way to extend that moment permanently. All I wanted was that feeling, all the time, nothing more.

"Buzzed Jay was no longer socially awkward or shy; he no longer cared about being an outcast; he wanted to be right in the center of the action and make himself known. He wasn't afraid of talking to the hottest girl or picking a fight with the biggest guy. He wasn't concerned with morals, or with being polite. Buzzed Jay was completely free, and at that time I felt that it was a good thing. Drunk Jay, on the other hand, was a little angry, forgetful and sloppy, and when you constantly chase a buzz, it never stops at a buzz.

"I should have noticed the warning signs early on, but I was too young and naïve. When Billy and KJ mentioned that I was getting a little out of control with the booze, I disregarded it as them just being pussies. They eventually started drifting away, and I never cared to even entertain the thought that I was the problem. When I started drinking before work in the mornings it was because my workload was getting stressful and the boss was an ass, and when I continued drinking at home after coming back from a party, it was because the drinks they were mixing were pretty weak. I had an excuse for everything. There were always reasons to drink, and then reasons to drink more.

"That night when Mom and Dad found me completely obliterated, spooning a half-empty bottle of Jim Beam in a bed soaked with my own urine, Mom said something that should have made me stop drinking immediately and never think about alcohol again. "I already lost someone to this! I don't want to lose you too!"

"It made me cry, but it didn't make me stop. A few years later I was relying on alcohol to blur every emotion, to deal with every decision. My life was falling apart and I didn't even notice. I went from job to job, not being able to hold on to one for longer than a month. I woke up hungover every single day, and if I hadn't had a drink by lunch time, I couldn't function well.

"Mom got tired of talking about it. She would walk in the room and pick up the empty bottles and cans dispersed all around, in quiet sadness and disappointment. Dad stopped talking to me, and the distance mounted between us. I didn't care, because I didn't feel, and if I didn't feel I didn't have to care.

"Years passed, and I slowly deteriorated physically and even more emotionally. I lost most of my friends, ruined my credit, my work history and my reputation. I became an anathema of a human being."

"Do you miss him?" Dr. Patel asked.

The question struck me as a bit odd. "Miss... who?" I asked. She didn't say a word.

"Well... he died when I was five so... I don't have a lot of memories of him."

"Do you miss him?" she asked again, wanting me to dig deeper and confront an emotion I had always repressed.

I lowered my head and closed my eyes. It took me some time to find the right thought, so well hidden it was deep inside my soul.

"I miss... the times we could've had together, the things I could have learned from him. I miss not being able to mourn him."

"They never told you he died..." she whispered.

"No." My eyes got moist.

"What did they say then?" she asked.

"That he went on a long work trip, then not much else. They thought I would forget as I grew up."

"But you didn't..."

"I did not," I replied.

"How did it make you feel?"

"Abandoned..." I uttered.

She allowed me a few moments to gather my thoughts. I wiped away the tears and she resumed writing on her chart. "Thanks Jay, we are making progress." Then she began the procedural questions:

"Any thoughts of hurting yourself or others? Are you seeing things or hearing voices that aren't there?"

"No…"

"Very good. Medication working well?"

"So far."

"Good, good, good." She wrote a last few notes. "I want you to start some of the therapy groups that we have available to you. Let's begin getting you ready to know how to deal with the issues in the real world."

I nodded in agreement as she dismissed me. When I got up and walked out of her office I felt like Neil Armstrong probably did when he took those first steps on the moon: light. It was interesting how a brief but deep conversation had brought me such sense of relief. The only other thing that could make me feel like this was intoxication. Why hadn't I done this instead? The answer immediately popped in my head as the image of my mother bending forward and under my grandfather's arm to guide him to bed appeared.

"Fear…"

CHAPTER 15

I found her sitting on the floor of the lounge, with her back against the wall where the broken clock hung, arms crossed and head down. She looked like a young child embracing the horrors of a well-deserved time out.

"Tara..." I called out. "May I join you?"

She looked up for a brief second - her eyes were swollen from crying; her face was red and puffy and her nostrils wet - then resumed her original position, while a few sobs escaped her breath. But she didn't say a word - for better or worse - so I bent down and sat beside her. Everything looked bigger from down there; the walls, the tables, the chairs. I felt like a six-year-old again, helpless against a giant world that could not be tamed. It made me wonder if Tara felt like this all the time, struggling with a reality that didn't understand her, living every day in a dimension that made sense to her but no one else, seeing things in a way that were logical only in her head. I thought about how overwhelming that existence could be, and I felt a deep sense of empathy for the girl. "I'm not mad at you, and I am sorry for throwing you off the bed. I hope I didn't hurt you. But you cannot do that again, Tara. It's disrespectful."

A gravelly voice came out from between her knees. "I'm sorry. I thought you liked me."

"I do, Tara. I think you are a nice girl, and I do want us to be friends." She slowly raised her head and looked up at me, reminding me of a golden retriever that knew it had done something wrong. "But friends, good friends, respect each other and their boundaries. Do you understand?"

She nodded her head in agreement. "I like friends." Her demeanor became more relaxed; she was now looking directly at me while a few tears found their path down her cheeks. She snorted loudly as she wiped her face harshly with her hand, wiping away water and snot, then drying the hand on her shorts. Her eyes lit up with expression, and although she didn't say a word, I could only imagine that she was already role-playing our future as best friends in her mind.

"Great!" I continued. "So what do friends have to do in order to be *good* friends?"

She was now as excited as the girl who would vigorously raise her hand in class when she knew the answer to the math problem the teacher had written on the board. "Respect boundaries, got it! Would you like to have a juice with me?"

"Sure…" I sighed. *I really hope Bob is right about this*, I thought. She jumped off the floor like a rocket and sprinted toward the nurse's station. "What now, Tara?" The nurse on the other side rolled her eyes at her. All the nurses on rotation where already aware of Tara and her shenanigans, but they treated her less like a patient and more like that hyperactive child who had to go to work with her parent because school was closed for the day.

"Jay and I would like some juice, please!" she said, while standing on her tippy toes for some reason.

"All right, but just because you asked nicely," the nurse smiled.

We sat at a table that was directly under flickering fluorescent lights. Usually, from what I had seen, there was a maintenance guy who took care of all the repairs needed on the floor – he was the one who put the phone box back to its righteous place after the gargantuan man ripped it off the wall – but the bad lights had gone unnoticed since I had gotten there. Tara said that it reminded her of a party she went to once, and she could hear the beat of the music through the rhythmic intermittence of the faulty lights.

She had a box of grape juice in her hand; I had orange. She opened the lid and took a quick whiff, then poured a few drops on the palm of her hand and tasted with a few licks. She seemed pleased. I took a few sips of my juice and she took a couple of hers. We sat in silence while the lights flickered, music played in Tara's head and she explored every inch of my face. It bothered me a little at first, to have her eyes so obnoxiously devoted to me, but I could tell that she didn't do it maliciously; she was just being true to who she was, quirky and curious and spirited, intrigued and engulfed in wonder by the most insignificant things.

"You have a Hayato heart," she said, with unusual confidence.

"I don't know what that means, Tara," I responded, as I took a sip of the juice and momentarily broke eye contact with her.

"Hayato was my fiancée; he loved me and I loved him. We were going to get married and move to Japan, close to his family. We never did."

"What happened?" I asked, curious.

"I messed it up. The third time I visited Japan he was finally willing to introduce me to his friends, and one night we all went out to sightsee around Tokyo. I was shy and nervous; I really didn't know how to act. I had never been that good around groups of people. They were all laughing and having a good time, speaking their language, which I couldn't understand. It felt like everything they spoke about was related to me. I began to get angry because they ignored me and laughed at me, and they wanted Hayato all to themselves. I felt abandoned, alone again, like when I was little, so I started to freak out and have a really bad panic attack. His friends laughed at me even more; they thought I was faking it for attention. I started to yell at them--I wanted to kill them! Hayato got really mad and didn't know what to do, so he grabbed me by the neck and started to choke me."

"Oh my God!" I had meant to say that in my mind but it escaped my mouth with a jolt.

"Oh, it's ok!" Tara smiled. "He apologized later. Their culture is a little different," she explained. "That's how they do things over there."

"Really, he told you that?" I asked, doubtfully and somewhat angry.

"Yeah! It would happen from time to time, when I would do something that would make him mad. Silly me, always making him angry... he would have no choice but to punish me, you know, so I would learn not to do it again. The bamboo rod he used to discipline me was painful, especially when he hit me in the back of the legs with it. But he did it because he loved me, because he wanted me to learn and get better. Sometimes he would lock me in the basement for a few days so I could think about what I'd done, and it worked! I would feel bad and never do it again. Oh! And this one time he got really mad and stabbed me with a pencil--see the mark here?" She pointed at her arm.

"Oh..."

"It was kind of funny, actually. He got angry because I... well I don't really remember but I did something stupid and he got really mad and stabbed me, but it's ok! He later apologized!" She was now grinning from ear to ear, and I could not find anything else to say, or the strength to say it. In her mind, she was this broken soul, this useless artifact that you would wind up every morning, and it would begin to mechanically march around the room, running into walls or furniture, not having the intelligence to recognize how to avoid obstacles, or choose where to go next. That's where people like Hayato would come in, and through fear, violence and torture, point Tara in the right direction, set her straight in her ways, and make her a better girl. This, of course, was a vile and dangerous way of thinking, but since it was all that Tara apparently knew, she had to somehow make sense of it in her own head.

"Hayato loved me and I loved him," she continued. "He was the first boy I kissed, you know. We went everywhere together--to the mall, the park, the fair. He wrote me love letters when he was away in Japan, and I loved writing him back. The things he said in those letters... the things he promised... I will never forget that, never. We were going to be together forever, and then, well, I screwed it up," she sobbed. "Why didn't his friends like me!" she snarled.

"Tara... it's ok," I said. "Try to calm down please; it's ok."

"Hayato had a good heart... I loved him and he loved me." That expression seemed to get stuck in her head, like a needle in a broken record, and she now kept repeating it as she manically shook back and forth on the chair. "I loved him and he loved me I and loved him and he loved me I loved him and he loved me I loved him... (she paused and took a large breath)

...and he loved me."

I had to do something to divert her attention or I thought she was going to snap and have another breakdown. "Tara, would you like more juice?"

"Sure!" Her memory was instantly wiped clean; she jumped off the chair and ran toward the nurse's station. Halfway through she paused and looked back at me. "You have a Hayato heart, Jay."

"Thanks, Tara. I will take that as a compliment," I smiled. But a complement it wasn't. In all honesty I didn't truly know if this Hayato character was real, or one person, or just a mix of different people that Tara had encountered in her life and had a devastating impact on it. I didn't know if she ever went to Japan, or if she was engaged at one point in time. I didn't know if she had ever kissed a boy or written a love letter. I knew nothing about her. I wasn't sure if the pencil mark was done by an angry Japanese man or she had done it to herself, but I did know one thing, and it was the most accurate conclusion that I could come up with:

This girl had suffered a great deal.

CHAPTER 16

"Mom likes to often recount the story of her labor, and how she spent twelve long hours in agony before I finally came into the world. She says that at one point during the struggle, a nurse jumped on her belly and pressed down to try to squeeze me out, and whether that's true or just a hallucination brought on by the hours of excruciating pain is beyond me.

"What Mom never talks about, however, is the fact that she lost two pregnancies before me. Her and Dad first conceived on their honeymoon, eager to get physical with each other after almost a year of supervised courtship, where they were barely able to hold hands. Seven months later she had a stillbirth, a baby boy they were going to name Eric. Two years later, after that loss became somewhat bearable, they decided to try again, and this time she gave birth to a girl, three months premature. They named her Sophia. She lived for two hours, thirty-two minutes and approximately forty-eight seconds. After that devastating blow Mom decided that her womb had now closed for good. But three years later, after a booze-filled anniversary celebration and a lack of contraceptives in the back of Dad's truck, they braced themselves for another harrowing loss.

"It was an utter coincidence that they met Dr. Gomez that day, when mom went for her first ultrasound appointment. He was taking some patients for Dr. Martiza, the young OB-GYN that Mom had been appointed to and who also happened to be his niece. Martiza was having an emergency of her own; her husband's antique Buick had broken down that morning, and finding basic means of transportation was one the biggest headaches that the Cuban regime had gifted its citizens. The old cars – antique Dodges and Chevrolets and Fords; relics from the forties and fifties when the US still had a presence in the island - had been modified through the years with whatever parts were available, and they required constant attention and maintenance. The Cuban men who had been fortunate enough to own one spent a great deal of their time keeping them alive and running. The cars would break down constantly and without warning, yet they were still more reliable than public transportation. Maritza had managed to call her uncle, who lived ten minutes away from the office, and he had agreed to take on a few patients so they wouldn't pile up on her. There is a high probability that if that old car had not broken down that day, I wouldn't have made it to tell the story.

"When Mom tells it, she makes sure to point out the fact that she does not believe in coincidences, and that the turn of events that transpired that day were the workings of a higher power. She had kneeled on the side of her bed every night, with fearful tears and broken heart, negotiating with God the terms of my arrival. She had promised to never miss church again, to help more in the congregation and dedicate more time to those with spiritual needs. Most importantly (and this was a big one for her) she was going to stop gossiping about others. She had an innate skill for storytelling, one that made her a favorite amongst the other women, who loved to hear the latest developments on the unhappy marriages, the sneaky husbands and the unsatisfied wives, the hypocrites and two-faced people of the congregation--the ones who acted one way in church and another on the streets, and so on and so forth. Mom had never felt more empowered than when she had all eyes pointing in her direction, waiting for her to start dishing out the goodies. It gave her purpose and made her feel valuable, something she hadn't really felt before, not to that level.

"To Mom, that day Dr. Gomez appeared in our lives and noticed on the ultrasound what no other doctor had noticed before, it meant that God was signing on the dotted lines and agreeing to the terms of the contract. Mom had an unusually short cervix, and whenever the fetus inside her grew to a certain size, it couldn't be contained inside the uterus. Dr. Gomez recommended a procedure where they would stitch the cervix shut, then she had to be on permanent bed rest, with feet elevated, for the rest of the term. Even then there were no guarantees, but she had a chance. I had a chance.

"A few months later there was (according to mom's account) a nurse sitting on her stomach, and I was being popped out like the cork of a champagne bottle. I always thought it was ironic that at first the risk was coming out too early, and then I didn't want to come out at all. *'Don't tell me that God doesn't have the power to open or shut all kinds of doors,'* Mom would boast while she recounted her miracle pregnancy, the one that finally gave her the most precious thing she'd ever owned.

"Most of the time when signing a contract, one usually forgets to read the fine print thoroughly, and I don't think that Mom even realized there was any when she held me in her arms. But there was, and whether she wanted to or not, she would eventually have to come to terms with that.

"When you are a young married couple with a brand-new baby, in a poor, socialist country, you usually don't have the means or opportunity to venture out and build your own nest. There is no real estate to be purchased; there is no land to build on. Everything is strictly managed and run by the government, which leaves you with very few options. Some couples gather up materials and build small rooms on top of their in-law's property, or simply move into a vacant bedroom, if there is one. That's how Dad and I ended up living in Mom's childhood bedroom, a few feet away from my grandparents. Dad didn't mind it though; he was easygoing enough to make it work through Grandma's controlling fits and Grandpa's drunken nights.

"There are several repercussions that come with being the one successful baby out of three, the main ones being overprotectiveness and fear, lots of fear. My parents always treated me like a fragile, porcelain doll that needed help walking, talking, playing and learning. Every activity was carefully monitored; no risks could be taken. Mom bathed me, fed me and even wiped my butt well into my tenth birthday. I was not allowed to play outside with other kids if they were not around, and I could never have sleepovers if one of them wasn't present. When I proposed that I was old enough to walk to school by myself, Mom gasped and said, "But, how are you going to know when to cross the street?" I was 11 years old.

"As fate would have it, the one thing they wanted me to do the least was the thing that I did the most, and what contributed, I'm sure, to my depressive issues early on. The overprotectiveness was not only physical, but also mental, where they wanted me to think in specific patterns, about specific things, without the slightest deviation. I came to the realization very early on that this was impossible for me to do. I thought about everything, obsessed even. There was no half-assed explanation that would satisfy me; things had to be logical, they had to make sense. Ideas and concepts had to fit together like pieces of a puzzle, and they had to have at least some basic evidence to back them up. But when you grow up in a world surrounded by religious fanaticism, not many things do. At same time, I was forbidden to express any doubts or ask any questions out loud, as that would only bring a scolding about *"how dare you question such matters, the very foundation of the rock we are standing on?"*

"My parents only noticed later, when it was already too late, that they had been alienating me since I was little. They did it harmlessly, not meaning any ill will. They just thought it was the right way to raise a child, and did the best they could with what little they knew. It affected me nonetheless; I never felt comfortable enough to express my true ideas, fears and opinions in front of them. I would've gotten shut down anyway. They never saw the real Jay, the vulnerable Jay, the child Jay. They only saw the person they wanted to see, the ghost I appeared to be. I felt like a fraud, the kid that would never grow up to his parents' standards, the ever-disappointing son. I was a failure, alone, misunderstood, and most of all, angry. I had dreams where I would yell at them at the top of my lungs, crying out for attention, for real understanding. They would always ignore me in the dream, which made me even angrier. I would wake up drenched in sweat and with tears on my face. Sometimes, when I'm able to dive into a deep sleep, I am still haunted by similar dreams, and I am reminded of how much I still struggle with.

"Mom sometimes says that she knows that what I've gone through is her fault, and it breaks her inside. She has this deep sense of guilt that she contends with on a daily basis, and although she accepts it, it makes her miserable. You would think she believes she went wrong by shielding me too much from the outside world or by doing the best in her power to not let me think on my own, but no. She thinks that she has gotten punished by God for not being able to keep her promise, and telling Olga that Veronica said that Mary only married Julio because he paid for her dad's hospital bill that day he had the heart attack on the way to Dina's wedding. That, and a few other slips of the tongue through the years, is what she is convinced brought the wrath of God down on our family, especially on me."

"Are you angry at God, Jay?" Dr. Patel asked.

She had the incredible skill of absorbing what I was saying and pointing out the problem areas. "Shouldn't the question be if I believe in God to begin with?"

"You can't be angry at something that you do not believe in," she replied.

I paused. It took me a moment to decipher my true feelings on the matter. I had to again go back through all the years of forced dogma and attempt to separate what I truly believed from what I was forced to believe. It was a challenging task to accomplish, since I had always learned that even doubting things in your mind could be a sin against the Holy Spirit, one that God might not forgive you for. But that fear had dissipated long ago for me, and it had been replaced by sadness, disappointment and, once again, anger.

"I'm angry at the way we appropriate God and use him as a crutch to not see what is right in front of us. I'm angry at the way we think God thinks, and how we express our own judgments through God's voice, as if he was a simple hand puppet. We use him to carry out our agenda, to instill our way of justice on others, to separate families, to create division, to hate. I'm not angry at God because I do not believe that God would approve of most things that people do in his name, because I see God through my eyes and no one else's."

"Isn't that also appropriation?" she asked. She knew how to make me stop in my own tracks and truly think about my feelings, my reasons and my logic. She didn't question me though, not in a way that I would doubt my opinions or my beliefs. She just wanted me to find my true self within me. She accurately reminded me that it was all just opinion based on experience, nothing more, nothing less. The way I saw things would never be one hundred percent accurate, just like my parents' way wouldn't, much less the rest of the world's.

I smiled. "Appropriation, huh... yes, Dr. Patel, you are correct. I know. I am really not as different from them as I think."

CHAPTER 17

Right behind the TV room was a small room that looked much like a kindergarten classroom, complete with coloring books, crayons, pencils, watercolors, rulers and board games. In one of the back corners there was also a box with cork-boards, play-doh, bingo cards and an assortment of colorful plastic balls, enough to make a pit out of the whole room.

The walls were decorated with drawings, watercolor paintings, crayon colorings and cutouts from previous students, most of them containing some sort of quirky motivational message, including but not limited to: *A POSITIVE MIND IS A POSITIVE LIFE, KEEP YOUR FACE TO THE SUNSHINE AND YOU CANNOT SEE A SHADOW, EVERY DAY BRINGS NEW CHOICES* and, my personal favorite, *JUST BECAUSE MY PATH IS DIFFERENT DOESN'T MEAN I'M LOST.* They were helpful reminders that the people who made them shared the same emotional struggles as the rest of us. It was as if they were reaching out through their art and putting a hand on our shoulders, silently reassuring us that it was going to be ok. This, of course, was not entirely true; a lot of the people who laid eyes on these walls would never be entirely ok; some of them wouldn't even come close. Then again, isn't that the case (in some fashion) for every single one of us?

I sat at the table closest to the window, hoping the sun would help me bear with the glacial temperature of the room. It was always chilly throughout the entire floor, but being confined to a small space where the cold air could not disperse quickly made it even worse. A few minutes later more patients began to gradually show up, occupying the rest of the empty chairs. Big Mike came in first, as always, playing with the comb in his hair. Donnie walked in right behind with notebook in hand, going on his usual tangent. He did a couple of laps around the room, found a spot of his pleasing, sat down, buried his head in the notebook and started to jot down the words that came out of his mouth, his hand having a hard time keeping up. He didn't give up, however, his fingers loosely wrapped around the pencil, dancing feverously with it as the lead generated almost incomprehensible words on the paper.

Donna the diabetic walked in after, and it didn't take long for everyone to notice that her green gown was undone, completely exposing her wide back, her corrugated buttocks and swollen legs. A couple of people groaned in disgust, and one lady even left the room while covering her mouth with her hand, trying to avoid regurgitating. In the background, you could hear the passive aggressive outrage of other patients, *C'mon Donna! Really Lady? Dude, that's disgusting! Can someone get this woman out of here?* Donna walked in with her head up - almost looking dignified - and calmly sat at an empty table, like she didn't seem to know what was happening or just wasn't bothered by it.

Tara barged in at her typical speed and, of course, sprinted for the chair next to mine. Even though she was bursting with the energetic excitement of a five-year-old girl, she didn't do anything that disrespected our newly established boundaries. She had a hard time sitting still, her leg constantly shaking and her hands always looking for new real estate to subdue. Bob also joined the table, sans Bible, such a permanent accessory of his that he looked like he wasn't wearing a shirt. Callie came in as well, looking a little strung-out. "The first few days are rough," she said in a coarse voice, answering the question no one asked but everyone thought. She sat down next to Bob and immediately put her head down on the table, her folded hands acting as support.

Maggie walked in last, stealthy as a ghost. She found a chair in the corner by the box with the balls, right under the air vent, where she knew no one would get close. She was always in flight mode, eyes wide open, scanning the territory like a bird of prey, ready to make an escape when necessary. She rubbed her hands vigorously on her thighs to make them warm, then she hugged herself by the waist to try to prevent some body heat from escaping, but the air vent didn't budge. She eventually moved to another table that hosted a couple of zombies, a valid alternative for complete solitude.

The morning sun crept through the window and its light spread gently across the tiny room. Outside, the foliage of the trees was thick and bright green, the leaves gently whistling in unison as the breeze cut through them. A slender old lady with white hair and an honest smile walked in, carrying a small boom box. "Hello everyone, my name is Peggy and I will be your instructor today... Donna, please go get that gown tied. Thank you. Okay! Let's get started then!"

She placed a box with mixed crayons on every table, as well as a stack of paper with the outline of a peacock printed on it. Her smile never disappeared as she walked around delivering materials. She was the embodiment of the quintessential grandmother character; her disposition brought a certain serenity to everyone in her presence; her sweetness was infectious, almost like she could make you feel better about anything, as long as she was nearby.

"Ok then!" she exclaimed. "As you can see, we are going to be coloring today, and while we do that we are also going to be enjoying some relaxing music, deal? All right, let's do it!"

She pressed the play button and the boom box started singing what sounded like eastern meditation music. Everyone grabbed a peacock, dug inside their crayon box and started coloring, while Peggy walked by the tables offering help and advice. "Callie, well done. Excellent use of the colors. Donnie, we are coloring *quietly* today; please stop talking or leave the room. Thank you. Tara, please don't press the crayons so hard; that is why they break. Bob, that Bible verse down there is very nice.

Jay..."

As the sun found its way to the center of the sky, a chunk of light above me rested on the table. I looked up and once again became enamored with the dust specks suspended in the air – like I had when I was a child - dancing with fabulous precision to the gentle beat of the music in the background. I wanted to interact with them but didn't know how. I thought about trying to hold one, but knew that was nearly impossible. I resigned to watching them move, and dance, and create patterns and become a small universe that maybe had life of its own. I felt a certain serenity connecting with my younger self by sharing the same thoughts, and feeling the same emotions. It made me feel like that young boy was still somewhere inside me, and I had full control of his well-being. I then continued coloring, making sure to stay within the lines, committed to making this peacock a piece of art, like the sun was committed to creating masterpieces out of the dust specks. I had forgotten how enjoyable it was to create and express so many interesting things through this medium.

I didn't remember what color peacocks or their feathers were, so I improvised. I used Sunset Orange, Melon, Laser Lemon and Electric Lime for the feathers, giving them Caribbean Green edges in contrast with a Turquoise Blue background. A little bit of Hot Magenta and Purple Pizzazz gave it the final touches, and by the time I was done I was quite pleased with the final product.

I later realized that I had been so focused on coloring that all background noise had dissipated, both inside and outside of my mind. The constant anxious state I found myself in had taken second place to the craft; it wasn't (hypothetically speaking) the loudest voice in my head. I got lost in a moment of pure enjoyment, in the simplicity of using my hands to give life to something new, something colorful and insignificantly special. I remembered, if only for a minute, the feeling. It was the swoosh through the net of the basketball hoop, the satisfaction of achievement, of doing something well, of having a smidgeon of value, something tangible that others could recognize as well. I was so submerged in it that I failed to hear Peggy calling out my name.

"…Jay?"

"Yes?"

"That's very nice work you've done there. Very nice work."

CHAPTER 18

We stood once again by the window, getting acquainted with the mid-morning version of the view. The sky was a shade of blue that refused to give the spotlight to the few clouds that freely roamed the stratosphere. The sun was at its warmest, and just putting a hand on the glass would momentarily soothe the penetrating shivers that gave us the polar temperature on this side of it.

In the distance, window cleaners rappelled down the side of buildings like Navy Seals. Impatient car horns made sure everyone stayed vigilant on the freeway, which was dead-stopped with heavy traffic. The parking lot below was seeing an influx of human and vehicular activity; people walking in and out of doctor appointments, probably getting bloodwork, taking x-rays, maybe getting a necessary wake-up call. They walked with an urgency that made it obvious that whatever they were doing was an interruption of their day; they needed to get in and out as quickly as possible so they could resume taking care of the things that really mattered. Not too far from where we stood a couple of small birds played, chirping away in happiness and intertwining in rhythmic cavort. Callie and I soaked up the view as we sipped on hot cups of coffee that they had available after lunch, to help those who wanted an upper hand in battling the drowsiness of the afternoon meds. I didn't have that problem, I just always enjoyed a cup of the black stuff. This one was particularly dull, but I didn't expect there to be Starbucks quality coffee on the psychiatric floor.

"Are you a pessimist, Jay?" Callie asked.

"Worse," I responded. "I'm a realist."

"Do you think we will ever be able to defeat these demons?"

"Depends on who you ask," I said. "An optimist would say yes. A pessimist would say no. Being a realist I have to say: I don't know."
She was visibly disappointed by my answer. "I wish I could just know for sure. I wish I was convinced it was worth it."

"You can only be sure of one thing, Callie, and that is that you will definitely fail if you don't try at all," I said, with a confidence that reminded me of those people on YouTube who pretended to be motivational speakers.

She paid close attention to the birds tussling on the other side of the glass. She followed every movement with her eyes, completely absorbed, as if she was watching a Broadway play. "My mother was a Playboy Bunny, you know, back in the sixties. Long-legged, beautiful Californian blonde. She met my dad on a trip she took to New York, at a bar in Manhattan. He was a handsome, muscular factory worker, with big ambitions and a bigger heart. He was sitting on a corner, sipping on his usual bourbon, when she walked in and ordered a Cosmo. He immediately recognized her, and two drinks later he built enough strength to go over and introduce himself. Daddy says it was love at first sight. Mom doesn't. Either way, they got married quick, six months after that day. He quit his job a few months later and began investing some of Mom's money into several ventures; he always had good business sense and worked very hard. Five years later he was on his way to building a manufacturing empire, and quickly expanded from New York to LA, and then overseas to the Philippines. Mom never had to work again.

"After I was born Mom became the typical housewife and Daddy continued to grow the business. Then my two brothers came along, Jake and Marlo. It wasn't a bad childhood initially, but Mom, not having much experience taking care of a home, would get easily overwhelmed and anxious having to handle everything by herself. I honestly think she really missed her Playmate years--the attention, the fame, the fact that every day was a surprise; you never knew what it was going to bring. She missed being young and vibrant and free, having something to constantly look forward to. And now there she was, playing house with a husband who was never home and three young kids. Every moment was scripted with the conspicuous boredom of a life that, like a video tape, would rewind at night and replay all over again the next day. So she started a habit of her own. She would take care of all the chores by six in the afternoon, and by seven she would have her first glass of wine. Two bottles later she would be passed out in bed, usually by nine. That routine also played over every single day, without exception, and with Daddy being at work until late at night, we were pretty much on our own all that time. Jake and Marlo were younger, and they were boys. Mom was all I had; she was the one person I could truly relate to, so I became very lonely." She took a sip of the now lukewarm coffee.

"There was a boy named Chad who lived right next door to us. Most afternoons, after Mom was in bed, Chad would sneak in through my bedroom window and we would play. I liked the company, even though I knew he wasn't that great. He was a couple of years older than me and had already earned a pretty devious reputation in school. A few times I had to stop his hands from touching forbidden places, but he was persistent and pushy, and it eventually paid off. I was afraid he would stop showing up and I would have to once again spend my afternoons in solitude. Then one day he brought a few pills he had stolen from his parents' medicine cabinet and told me to take one. I was confused. I told him I wasn't sick," she chortled. "I was so innocent back then. He said that it wasn't that kind of pill and told me to trust him. I took one, he took two, and just like that, it all began. As soon as that pill kicked in and the feeling traveled through my body, I fell in love with the high, more than I have ever loved a man--or anyone, in fact. That day Chad had his way with me and I didn't care. I didn't care that he fondled me and raped me and made me bleed pretty bad, that he choked me to the point that I almost fainted and that he left bruises all over my body. It didn't matter, because to me that day had been a gift. From that moment, I started chasing the feeling that pill gave me, and I haven't stopped ever since.

"A few years later, getting through High School was simple. It was easy for the daughter of a model to use her genetic advantages to get whatever she wanted. It always worked on the guys who had access to the drugs I wanted. When I graduated and went to college, Daddy put me on the payroll for the company, so I would automatically receive a paycheck every month to pay my expenses. He said that his little girl would always be taken care of, and he meant it. He wanted me to have what he never did. It was enough money to feed a family of four, but my roommate and I would live on ramen noodles and pasta, so we could spend the rest of the money on cocaine for her and pills for me. It was a crazy time.

"First overdose happened at twenty-two. I was on three 80mg Oxys and, I don't remember exactly, but at least four Xanax bars. Then came rehab, and then my first suicide attempt. My life took such a sharp turn, so quick, that I initially had a very hard time accepting it, but a few months later I was getting better, or so I thought anyway.

"Then for a while I was free again, and after a year Daddy restored my payroll checks, thinking I was ok. I was twenty-five when I met Phil, another pill junkie, and long story short, we enabled each other in the messiest of relationships, until he died next to me, overdosed on Vicodin. Then came another suicide attempt" – she took a sip – "but when you develop such a tolerance for pills, it's kind of hard to accurately decipher how many are going to kill you.

"I moved back in with my parents and tried to keep it straight for a while, failed miserably. Ended up in rehab again, and again after that. That's when Daddy completely cut me off for the first time, so I had to resort to using my genetic advantages again and started stripping. By that time, the habit got so expensive that dancing wasn't enough, so I started taking clients home after shifts. I became a full-service escort; I would provide the sex, they provided the drugs. Got arrested a couple of times for solicitation, and got raped more than once." As she raised the Styrofoam cup to take another sip of coffee her hand shook, while a tear barely missed falling inside of it. "It was a dark time, Jay, a dark time."

"Callie, I'm so sorry," I said, with sadness.

"And now I'm here," she managed a haggard smile. "Daddy is negotiating my admittance to a facility in Orlando, The Sunrise Center. They want a fifteen-thousand-dollar deposit; Daddy wants to bring it down to ten. He's a great businessman, he'll get it done," she said, finishing what was left of her the coffee.

"And then?" I asked.

"And then another attempt at making better choices, and I have the feeling this chance is my last," she said.

"I know you can do it," I said, earnestly.

"I thought you were a realist!" she laughed.

"Indeed," I replied. "If I am to believe that I can do this, Callie, I have to believe that you can do it too."

Her eyes softened at the thought of doing something truly remarkable for the first time in her life. The concept of sobriety for Callie was as far-fetched as unicorns and lake-dwelling dinosaurs, so achieving it, to her, was achieving the impossible. Yet the impossible had never seemed so plausible as just now. We both stayed in silence for a while, watching the flirtatious birds that continued to dance against a backdrop of perfect sky. It was almost as if they knew that they were being watched and wanted to put on a great show for us.

"Do you ever think we will be as free as them?" Callie asked.

"Birds are only as free as their instincts allow them to be, and so are we," I said, proving to her how much of a realist I really was.

"Yet they can fly, and we can't," she uttered.

We stood by the big window until the small birds retreated to their nest, on the tree by the light pole, in the parking lot below. Callie headed to the phone box to get an update on her transfer and I went to battle the broken clock.

Maybe we weren't that free after all.

CHAPTER 19

He was born to a humble family of four and raised in the outskirts of the city of San Cristobal, in the Dominican Republic. His father was an aspiring musician once, playing keys for a small merengue group in clubs throughout Santo Domingo, hoping to one day make it to one of the bigger, more recognized ensembles that were popping throughout the island. When that dream faded, the old man resigned to working as a waiter in a small café, where he made just enough to put food on the table and not much else.

Yet Tony had learned a lot from his father when it came to making a living. "Whatever you do, you got to do it well and proud," he would tell his son occasionally, when he would come home from an arduous double shift, bathed in the stench of burger meat, French fries and resignation. "No matter what, Tony, you got to do it proudly," he reiterated.

When his sister moved to the United States with her husband (an aspiring baseball player) in '93, Tony, filled with possibility, began to dream. "Maybe I will be able to go to a Cubs game someday," he pondered, Sammy Sosa being his idol at the time. There were magazine cutouts and posters all over the room he once shared with his sister, and when he lay in his bed late at night, the pictures would come to life; Sosa hitting another homer, the ball jumping out of the page as he rounded the diamond, or making a leap in right field to end an inning with loaded bases, or shifting his head to look at Tony dead in the eyes and giving him his signature "backwards" peace sign, smiling, as if saying *I'll see you soon*. It was 1997 when that dream got a closer to reality, after a family reunification visa allowed Tony and his parents to move to the US with his sister. By then the hope of the Big Leagues was dead, and so was her marriage. Her husband had become more passionate about cocaine and hookers than about the game, and he ended up having a heart attack that didn't kill him, but benched him permanently from the sport, as well as his sexual deviances. As a recently divorced and bitter woman, she now waited tables at a coffee shop in Little Havana, and a couple of days a week she cleaned the house of some wealthy clients she had met at the restaurant. She only got paid for the maintenance of the mansion, but found herself playing the role of babysitter, cook and even therapist to a middle-aged, bored, rich housewife several times a week. It was exhausting and sometimes a little disparaging, but she had to do what she had to do. The parents would most likely have to do the same: find some menial hospitality job that paid less than minimum wage, work double shifts, offer great service to generate decent tips and, little by little, start making their way up in their new home. So the years passed, and Tony began to gradually lose his enthusiasm for the Cubs and began to dream about going to a Marlins game.

Having parents who had no choice but to both work long hours meant that Tony would sometimes spend entire days alone, waiting earnestly for someone to come home, someone he could talk to, a voice that would fill the silence that sometimes drove him to the brink of insanity. He decided to make himself useful when he was not at school, and learned how to cook, iron clothes, mop the floors and dust the furniture. By the time his exhausted mother would get home, most of the chores in the house were already done. It had always brought a smile to her face--not the fact that he had done so much, but that he had done it out of his own sense of responsibility, without her having to ask. After he graduated from high school, Tony decided to start contributing financially by working full time to help with the bills, but his dad was not thrilled with that choice and flat out forbade it. "Tony, we don't waste opportunities," the old man instilled in him. "Being in this country is the biggest opportunity a man can have, and you will take advantage of it." Over the course of the years, his dad had saved every penny he could and left the funds untouched in a secret account that not even Tony's mom knew about. The day that he graduated with a nursing degree, Tony knew that it wasn't money that had paid for it; it had been resilience and sacrifice, and an almost supernatural determination to see your children succeed. It hadn't been his ideal choice, nursing, but baseball wasn't at all realistic and a nursing degree paid well and didn't take long to get. After finding out that phlebotomy was not a strong suit, Tony opted to specialize in the mental health branch, where being accurate with a needle was not as important as in other areas. A couple of years later, he was officially a psychiatric nurse, and he now roamed the halls of Memorial Hospital with clipboard and flashlight in hand, monitoring patients, breaking up scuffles, helping with sedation and bringing in the food carts. It was work that kept him constantly busy, but he liked that. It made the hours pass by like a breeze, and before he knew it he was out of there, feeling tiredly satisfied about his performance that day.

Having the same native language and coming from similar cultures (where baseball and music rule the streets and a smile doesn't cost anything) can create a visceral connection between two people, and that's exactly what happened with Tony and me. That very first night of visitation he had heard me speak Spanish to my parents, and when they left he came over and asked where I was from. "Cuban, huh," he said in his strong accent. "I grew up with Cubans in Miami; those are my brothers right there." He sat at the table across from me, waiting for the remainder of the visitors to disperse and keeping an eye on the patients who were left behind. Sometimes a glimpse of separation anxiety could take hold of some of them and make them act erratically, and Tony was the one responsible for keeping things under control. We talked for a while, about our childhoods and struggles we faced, about music and sports and the intoxicating lines of the body of a Latin woman, the ones that could bring any man to his knees, no matter how strong he thought he was. We talked proudly about parents who sacrificed what little they had for the benefit of their children, and *how much we put them through in exchange*, I added, feeling a legitimate sense of remorse, knowing that I was one of the most at fault. We then laughed aloud, noticing the similarities of our upbringings and the disciplinary tactics of all Hispanic mothers. Once the conversation allowed for some momentary silence to creep in, came the question that begged to be asked. "Jay, que tu haces metido aqui?"

"Look around you, bro," he said, "There are people here who have no idea they are here. This place is not for you. Bouts of depression can be treated with medicine and therapy, out there. Addiction can be treated with therapy and counseling. Out there. These place is reserved for those who can no longer be helped, only looked after. Try not to end up here again."

"We didn't know where else or who else to turn to, my parents and me. I'm making the best out of it, Tony, and then we'll see," I countered.

"You have to wake up every day and thank the heavens that you have what you have," he added. "Look at you: decent-looking guy, smart, well presented. Look at all that, all you have. Do you know what that is, do you know what that truly is, Jay?"

"What?" I asked.

"Opportunity," he responded, "and I learned a long time ago that you do not waste opportunity."

I nodded, knowing that he was right. We continued our conversation, discussing a much better future and the potential he saw in me. He told me stories of other patients and all the unhinged behavior that he had witnessed throughout the years: people who were really ill with a darkness that forced them to live in a parallel, yet much crueler reality. Without realizing it we had made the transition to our mother tongue and we had been speaking it for a while.

"Excuse me... ahem, excuse me..." a voice interrupted the conversation.

"What is it, Tara?" Tony asked, annoyed.

"I was taught that it is very rude to speak in a language that not everyone present understands. Please talk in English. Thank you."

"You know what, Tara..." He held himself back before saying something he knew he would later regret. "I was taught that you do not interrupt conversations that you are not invited to be a part of, so please get out of my presence."

She pulled a long face while she stared deep into Tony's eyes, a conspicuous attempt at establishing dominance. But before saying another word, Tara realized that this was not a battle worth fighting, so she walked away with shoulders down, hypothetically flying her white flag. I chuckled in between breaths, having found the whole scuffle pleasantly hilarious.

That night after I went to the big window with Callie and then stumbled into my room in a Seroquel-induced coma, Tony continued his clipboard work by making sure everyone was accounted for, and then going room by room, shining lights in faces and making checkmarks. The night was his favorite time of the shift, his thoughts mostly his, the repetitive tasks allowing his brain to work on more important things while it was engaged on autopilot.

His shift ended at five in the morning and he drove straight home, eager to get there quickly. He jumped in the shower and washed the night away, put a on a new set of scrubs and went to the kitchen. He cooked and ate scrambled eggs in the dark (his favorite) and drank a couple cups of coffee to get a bit of strength back. He threw the dishes in the kitchen sink after he was done, with the honest intention of washing them later. But he couldn't do it; he couldn't let them sit there, procrastinating, when he knew he could take care of them so quickly. After washing and drying them thoroughly, he put them in the cabinet above the sink and headed to the master bedroom.

"How's he doing today, Mom?" he asked as he gently knocked on the room and cracked the door open.

"He slept ok," she said, with a tired grin. She sat in a recliner next to a bed that held a withered body, mostly bones and skin, eyes sunken in and yellow skin. Tony walked in, leaned over and kissed his mother tenderly on the forehead. "Good night," he said, keeping a careful eye on her as she got up and left the room. He then changed the catheter bag, checked vitals and sat down in the recliner his mother had previously occupied. He reached forward and, as he grabbed his father's fragile hand, he saw his childhood projected on the canvas of a cadaveric face that could no longer give advice. He went back to those days in the Dominican Republic, lying on his bed, looking at the pictures on the walls, except this time they weren't posters of Sammy Sosa hitting homers or catching flyballs. They were of a man, weathered and tired from long hours at work, sitting next to a young child, talking, saying important things that brought Tony a great sense of peace, intertwined with nostalgia. He tried to let go of his father's hand to lean back on the recliner, but the old man's grip had tightened and would not let go. He surrendered a bitter smile and brought the captive hand toward his face, kissing the part that belonged to his dad and moving it to his cheek in order to capture a rogue tear. Then Tony realized that his father had been wrong all along; coming to America was not the biggest opportunity that life had given him. No, in fact, it had been being the son of that old man that now wasted away in that bed, but not without doing what he had to do first, and doing it proudly.

CHAPTER 20

Dear Viewer,

We interrupt your regularly scheduled programming to bring you this public service announcement: Addiction, what it is, how it affects you and, most importantly, is there hope? I am your host Jay Rodriguez, and in the upcoming minutes we will explore these questions and more, giving you direct access to the inner workings of a brain that refuses to let go of the very substances that threaten to destroy it. Don't go anywhere. We'll be right back.

I drifted through the halls of the psychiatric floor at a steady pace, seeing a man in cargo shorts and a black shirt who looked through the lens of a professional video camera that pointed at me, to his right a young woman with headphones holding a boom mic over my head. I always wondered what it would be like to be on TV, everybody knowing your name, or at least who you were--perhaps the local celebrity that brings that special news report every Friday, the one that exposes issues in the community: *businesses exposed for mistreating or scamming clients, growing concerns with gang violence in schools, the local government refusing to look into the quality of the drinking water.* I sometimes imagined pushing a cart at the grocery store, or maybe walking into a movie theater, while a couple stood barely in range of my peripheral vision, trying to decipher amongst themselves, *Hey, isn't that the guy from TV?*

Sometimes severe boredom can make you do silly things.

There was activity on the floor and I didn't care. In a previous state of mind I would have been absolutely terrified and self-aware, the fear of judgmental, critical and devious eyes heading in my direction, immobilizing me physically and crippling me emotionally. But I didn't feel like that around these people, not because many of them did not have the mental capacity to understand, much less chastise me for what I was doing, but because they had so many challenges of their own and so many things to contend with in their own dimensions, the least abnormal thing they saw was me. If I was to play pretend, this was the one place to do it without the fear of being judged, much less noticed, and I liked that. I liked the fact that I could be myself, act like myself and feel like myself at any time, without feeling like I was disrupting the time-space continuum, deviating from a carefully mapped out agenda that I was supposed to strictly follow if I wanted to be considered a normal and valuable member of society. Most people here had no agendas, could not fit into the social construct even if they wanted to, and the last thing they were worried about was how they were being perceived by others. In a bright stroke of irony, I felt safer in here than I did out there.

The cameraman holds up four fingers, mouthing the words.

Three...
Two...
One...

Black screen. The word ADDICTION fades in, then fades out. Another sentence appears.

Noun. The fact or condition of being addicted to a substance or activity.

Fade to black. Three second duration, and...

Action!

I look at the camera.

Addiction is a problem of epidemic proportions. In the United States alone, over 20 million Americans past the age of 12 have an addiction, and more than one hundred people die every day from drug overdoses. This rate has tripled in the past 20 years. It is reported that almost 7 million people who suffer from addictions also have a mental illness.

I keep my pace as I walk through the hall, audibly talking to an invisible camera. Some patients close in, slightly interested in who or what I am talking to, as if worried about the fact that I am seeing something that they are not. It's not the fact that I'm seeing it that worries them, it's the fact that they aren't. I am wearing a white, slim fit, long sleeve shirt with black slacks and a thin black tie. My sleeves are rolled up, a Movado watch hangs from my left wrist and my hair is gelled to perfection, combed to the right, a thin line splitting it downward on the left side of my head. I keep my hands in front of me, my fingertips touching, making a crude triangle. As I talk I make slight gestures to accentuate what I am saying, but not enough to take attention away from it. I feel like I've been doing this my entire life.

Those are the cold hard facts, the facts that most mental health professionals are aware of. But those facts do not tell us much about the disease itself, who it affects, how much, and, of course, what we asked early on: is there hope?

I can't tell you much about what physically goes on in the brain of an addict as I am not a neurologist, and the field of Neurology itself has a lot of work to do in the study of addiction. Neither can I comment on the demographics, as I am not a statistician, and many addicts are not open about their problem, making the job of accurately assessing the numbers much harder. What I can, however, offer you, is direct access to the destructive behavior of an addict, through the eyes, ears and heart of an addict.

The camera pans to the left and there is now a young boy sitting on the edge of a single-wide bed next to me. He is wearing a plain wife beater, basketball shorts and flimsy flip flops. His feet dangle from the bed as if he was on the edge of a precipice, considering whether to jump or not. Everything goes dark and a spotlight concentrates on him. He is looking down in shame, hands on his lap, not saying a word.

Meet Jay. He is nine years old. His entire life has been filled with fear, anxiety and grief. He has no friends and little, if any, self-esteem. He is bullied at school and misunderstood at home. He has little hope for the future and cannot understand his world. There is no one to guide him because no one has taken the time to really get to know him; they just follow the scripts they are given and ignore the innate desire to think for themselves. Jay will make it through his early years, but barely (the image of the young boy fades out and there's now an adolescent sitting on the bed with the same head-down position) *The sadness and lack of self-worth that consume him are no longer a part of him, they ARE him. He thinks this is the way it will always be, until…*

An unidentified hand reaches into the spotlight and gives the young man a red cup. He grabs it warily, briefly studies it and takes a whiff. His face crumples in disgust as he extends his arm to get the cup as far away from his face as possible, his senses alarmed and safeguarded. But the same hand slowly pushes the cup back toward him. He winces, hesitates momentarily, then shrugs. *What the hell,* he whispers and takes a sip.

His pupils instantly dilate and he extends his neck to look around with newfound curiosity and wonder. The spotlight gradually expands and morphs into daylight, shining bright on everything he sees. Colors distort and appear brighter, all shades of blues and greens and violets. He stands up and, with unusual courage, begins to speak in a loud and unrestricted tone of voice, letting everything out that has collected inside through the years: all the pain, the anger, the fear. The weight that has kept him down all along begins to disappear. There is a listening ear, someone who understands, somewhere, either inside or outside of him, yet he doesn't know who. Grateful tears of happiness and enlightenment emerge, the young man realizing that he is feeling something he has never felt before: comfort. Something or someone is spreading their arms and embracing him in the inexplicable warmth and peace of fearlessness, and he welcomes it, like young chicks welcome the warmth and safety of their mother's wings.

The camera now focuses on the white shirt, black tie version of me. *Since that day, Jay knows that he has found a true friend and confidant in alcohol. He is now receiving a type of sympathy he hasn't gotten before, and he does not want to ever let that go.*

Is it necessarily a bad thing that this young man has discovered something to help him potentially cope with his troubles? Is it a sin to rely on something to make life a bit more bearable? No, not necessarily, but Jay has yet to understand that alcohol is not a friend, no, alcohol is a god, and like most gods, it requires exclusive devotion.

The scene again changes and the spotlight shines on the bed, exposing a man lying in the fetal position, spooning a half empty bottle of Vodka. A haggard old couple stands over the bed. The woman, weak and battered, sobs and falls to her knees. She extends her arms and angrily shakes the body that lies under the sheets, but it won't react, not because it's dead, no. This is much worse than that. She screams at the top of her lungs, her tears flooding the floor until there is no more to cry from. She grabs the bottle of vodka, and with what little strength she has left throws it against the wall, shattering it into a million pieces of desperate sadness and broken soul. There is no reaction. The man standing next to her bends down and lovingly helps her up, hugs her tight, and replaces her in crying the tears she cannot cry anymore. He holds her by the waist to support her as they leave the light, crippled with resignation.

The young man now sits on the bed, looking more alive than he did previously, but still flushed and puffy, his eyes lost and out of focus, his body stooped and unstable. A young girl walks in, pretty, long hair, kind face, but exhausted. He stands up in a sloppy motion that makes him almost fall over, but manages to stay on his feet to wobble close to her, and begins to yell frantically, while holding another bottle of Vodka in one hand. The girl yells back for a few seconds, then starts to cry, defeated and tired. He yells harder and puts an index finger in front of her. There is slobber all over his mouth, sweat emerging from every pore, and premature wrinkles drawing grim lines on his face. He pauses, lifts the bottle and begins to chug, trying not to lose the courage that he needs to continue on the offensive. She angrily shoves him, hard, and he falls back on the bed. As she runs away, scared and brokenhearted, he begins to laugh maniacally, having successfully accomplished his goal of destroying everything around him.

He stumbles back on his feet, takes another chug and looks in front of him. His eyes widen and moisten while his face fills with anger. The camera moves and positions itself behind him, showing what he sees in front of him: a mirror with his pitiful reflection painted on it. A fist drives into the glass and shatters it. The spotlight goes off. Perfect-hair Jay stands in front of the camera.

What is addiction? Its exchanging control of one's life in return for momentary comfort; it is giving up the potential of a future for a present without fear. It is giving up everyone you love as retribution for something that seems to understand, and yet, it is still not enough. You also must physically and emotionally destroy the ties that bind you and your loved ones, making sure that they will never again become a priority. You must then worship this cruel god more and more every day, even though every day it gives you less and less.

The spotlight turns on one last time to shine on a disheveled man, bearded, naked and dirty. He wears scrapes, scabs, dirt, dried up blood, bites and bruises as decoration, irrevocable proof that his body has stood the test of the worst that life can throw at a human being, but barely, and not for much longer. His eyes are empty and without emotion, his face is pale and sickly. He holds another bottle of vodka in his hand, almost empty now. A couple of rats circle around him, lurking between his legs, nibbling on the dead skin from his feet. There is a constant drop of water that falls next to him, and he positions himself close enough to it so it falls in his hand, so he can use it to somewhat hydrate. There is a shackle on his right foot that chains him to an iron ball that grows bigger every few minutes or so, as if by magic, like a balloon being inflated by the clown at a birthday party.

Addiction is complete surrender, a sacrifice in exchange for the comprehension, acceptance and sympathy you have not received before, the one you've never felt within you, the self-love that you cannot grow inside you. Addiction takes it all and then demands more. When you are out of payment options, it will discard you like the casino discards the broke gambler and tosses you out into the cold.

Black tie Jay talks directly at the camera, in perfect contrast with the man who was previously seen.

Back to the question we asked at the beginning of the program: is there hope?

There is a pause and my eyes go deep inside the lenses. There is silence for a while. The cameraman makes desperate hand gestures, begging me to say something. The girl holding the boom mic begins to glisten with anxiety as the mic trembles above my head. But I don't know what to say; I am at a loss for words, realizing that I don't even know the answer to that question. Reality sets back in; the frigidness of the floor crawls back inside me, as I realize that I am no longer wearing long sleeves and slacks.

Unfortunately, that is all the time we have for today. We will have to explore that question further and try to find the answer in our next episode. We now return you to your regularly scheduled programming.

CHAPTER 21

I met Devon during dinner my third night in the joint. It was another "lovely" afternoon, and Tara had willingly saved me a "special" seat next to her at the table under the flickering lights. Feeling the need to have some type of buffer between us, I had asked Bob if he could join, but he insisted that he could not read his Bible under those ridiculous lights, although I knew the real reason was that he could only tolerate Tara a few minutes at time. I looked around for Callie, but she never came out of her room. The world was still spinning a little too fast for her, and having anything in her stomach to twirl along with her brain would only make it worse. So even though Devon's presence was unexpected, it was not unwelcomed at all.

He was a young black man who looked to be maybe in his early twenties. His physical characteristics, like the short stature, the slanted eyes and protruding tongue made it difficult to assess his real age, but he was no kid. He was sharply dressed in a striped shirt, cargo shorts, white tube socks that went up close to his knees and New Balance sneakers that looked as new as they day they were made. His feet swung fervently on the chair, not being able to reach the floor, and if I was to guess, Devon preferred it that way. He was intently focused on the food tray that he had in front of him - his eyes scanning and studying every item, a little bit of drool escaping his mouth, as the weight of his tongue on his lower lip kept it slightly open – but he wasn't eating. It was back to cheeseburgers and stale fries that night, and Devon did not seem too thrilled about it.

"Jay, this is Devon. He just got here a few hours ago," Tara said, while carrying out her own detailed observation of the food.

"Nice to make your acquaintance, Devon," I greeted him with a firm yet pleasant handshake. His eyes parted ways with the food momentarily, and he looked at me with a smile, a smile like I hadn't seen before, pure as spring water, honest, without ulterior motive or agenda. I had never experienced such transparency, not even in younger children. Devon had no secrets; he was an open book that kept being written as the days came and went, and he welcomed you to be a valuable contributor to his story. Being in his presence felt as refreshing as that last afternoon breeze that arrives from the sea accompanied by the sunset, leaving you with messy hair and a picture-perfect memory. His smile was unadulterated and true, missing the flaws and the conniving nature of the rest of humanity. I had not experienced anything like Devon's smile before.

"Hi," he said in a slurred voice that was hard to comprehend, not that it mattered; his smile said more than his words ever could. I became very interested in this peculiar young man, convinced that he had something unique and incredibly special from which I could learn. So while the clock chased down the minutes and we quietly sat in the presence of crudely prepared food, I began asking him basic questions: where was he from, did he have any siblings or pets, what was his favorite thing to do. His answers were sometimes short, other times indecipherable, and on some occasions, he didn't even answer. He would simply look away from the food and grin, traveling to a specific place in his mind that always made him happy, instantly transferring that emotion to the ones who were close by. The more Devon spoke and the more he smiled, the more invested I became. Even Tara seemed to be affected by Devon in some way; her signature paranoia had taken a back seat and she quietly sat at the table, enjoying the back-and-forth interaction he and I had going on.

After dinner ended and we parted ways, I decided to go back to the TV room and catch a glimpse of the basketball game before swinging by the pharmacy to take the Seroquel. It wasn't late enough for me to go to sleep, and lying in my bed with Bob beside me would usually bring an impromptu Bible lesson that I usually didn't mind hearing; I just wasn't in the mood tonight. The TV room was empty so I grabbed the remote, made my way to the back row and sat down in a corner seat, putting my feet on the backrest in front of me. The plastic chairs were bolted to the floor and rigid, cold and corrugated, lacking all the aspects that make a chair comfortable. But if you positioned yourself just the right way – feet resting on the backrest, slightly curled on your stomach and turned about twenty degrees to the left – it was barely tolerable. I began to press the up button on the remote repeatedly, looking for the station that was broadcasting the NBA finals. The Cavs were leading the series 2-1; if Curry didn't show up for this one Lebron would be almost impossible to defeat in game 5.

I had to circle through the stations a couple of times, the commercials not letting me figure out what channel I was looking for. When I finally found it, the game had just begun; they were five minutes into the first quarter and James had six points, Curry three. The Warriors had home court advantage and Golden State was making sure to make itself known. It was loud, a sea of blue and gold bouncing up and down like a wave in high seas, those long skinny balloons shaking madly behind the free-throw courts. The camera would cut to the stands occasionally, showing kids and adults with painted faces and cardboard signs, pretty girls dancing in their seats with a drink in hand when the play was stopped, and the occasional baby that a parent would lift up over their head (very much like Simba at the beginning of The Lion King), everyone begging for the camera's attention. The crowd became that valuable sixth player on the court; the motivating force with the power to drive underdogs to make miracles and to win championships.

I got so (surprisingly) involved in the action that for a while I failed to notice the small silhouette that quietly stood under the arch of the front door, exploring the room, as if assessing the risks of walking in. At first, I thought that Devon was roaming around trying to get acquainted with the psychiatric floor, having recently gotten there and all. Later I found out that he was already well acquainted; this wasn't his first or his second rodeo. Seeing him standing there in absolute silence creeped me out a bit, and for a little while I wasn't sure if I should acknowledge his presence or just pretend I didn't see him. I kept watching the game, periodically shifting my attention toward the door, curious to see what he would do next. There was finally an instance where he caught me looking, and when he realized that I had noticed his presence, his signature smile appeared, almost letting me know that this was the moment he was waiting for. "C'mon in, Devon, watch the game with me," I asked, all my concerns having disappeared after making eye contact with him.

He walked in with visible excitement and sat next to me. The first quarter wound down and the Warriors were keeping it close. If they kept the pressure on defense and the crowd kept the energy, they had a chance. From time to time I would use my peripheral vision to check on Devon, who still sat quietly to my right, still trying to find the sweet spot on the uncomfortable chair. I noticed that for the most part he wasn't really paying attention to the TV, instead he was paying close attention to me, and *my* reactions to the game. He waited for my next display of emotion, whether that was amazement at an impressive play or disappointment at a missed scoring opportunity. He read every eye twitch, every forehead line. Even when I got a little teary-eyed watching a sad life insurance commercial, Devon paid attention. My excitement, no matter how mild, was immediately registered by Devon, and he mirrored it by grinning and gently rocking back and forth on the seat. When I showed concern or disappointment, he would turn his head to the TV to explore the reason why, then he would look at me, impatiently waiting for the bad to go away and for another influx of excitement to emerge. When it would finally happen, he would again rock back and forth on the seat and grin so wide that it would make his eyes almost squint shut.

We stayed there until half-time, when the need to sleep then became my priority. I told Devon I was going to take my medicine and call it a night. He said what I can only imagine meant "me too," and he walked with me all the way to the pharmacy door and waved goodnight. Watching his small shadow disappear behind him as he entered the darkness of his room, I felt like I had made a good choice by skipping the Bible lesson and hanging out with Devon instead.

The next morning at breakfast, I saw Devon and Tara sitting under the flickering lights, and I was glad to know that I would be welcomed at their table, so I grabbed my tray and sat down with them. Tara was having issues with her boiled egg; she was concerned that the animal that laid it hadn't been a chicken, and eggs laid by bunnies are not supposed to be eaten; they're supposed to be colored and hidden for children to find. I managed to convince her that I had worked at a chicken farm a few years back, and I had no doubt that a chicken had laid that egg, plus it wasn't even close to Easter time, the only time bunnies were known to lay eggs. She ate the thing without further questions as Devon looked on in amusement, and I thought about how proud Jerry would have been of me. After the trays left the table, Devon pulled a few papers and a couple of crayons out of his pocket and began to draw. Tara got up to chase down the director, who she saw making his morning rounds. Maybe she had new complaints for him, or she was just giving a detailed report on her super-spy work. Devon and I sat at the able, and this time I was the one paying close attention to him and his work.

I noticed that he continued drawing the same thing on every single sheet of paper, and he now had several finished works spread out on the table. They were calendars, all of the month of March, but different years, starting with 1992 and going up. "That's nice work you are doing there, Devon," I complimented him.

"Thank you," he smiled.

My mild curiosity grew. As I began to make assumptions in my head about Devon's infatuation with the days and the month, I figured it would probably be easier to ask some probing questions, instead of letting my imagination go wild. "So, you like the month of March, I see."

"Yes," he grinned.

"Let me guess... it's your birthday?"

"No. It my friend birthday."

"Oh, your friend's birthday. Very cool. And you are drawing him... calendars?" I asked, with a hint of confusion.

"No," he replied. "They for me."

"Ok, ok…" I tried to little by little put together the pieces. "So you are drawing calendars of your friend's birthdate because he is having a party?"

"No," he said. "I do party for my friend. Every year. Last year I forgot and he mad. Now I don't forget."

For a while I sat in front of Devon under the faulty lights, which surprisingly didn't seem to bother him while he drew. He finished calendars on all the sheets he had with him, then found Peggy and went with her to the classroom behind the TV room to get more. He drew calendars from March 1992 all the way to March 2076, eighty-four in total. It took him close to two hours – which I spent the most of just quietly watching -- and when he finished, he took them and rolled them in his hand, got up, waved at me with a satisfied grin and walked away. "Nap time. Bye." He could now rest assured that he wouldn't repeat his mistake in the past, present or future, and his friend could no longer be mad.

I had an epiphany at that moment. I had been very wrong about Devon. It wasn't his smile that was pure and honest, and unlike any other smile on the planet (filled with secrets and lies and hate, and envy and jealousy and superficiality). This young man had something that was indescribable and special, a type of simple understanding of how the world worked, the rudimentary basics that kept things spinning, and that made it easy for him to find a way to be happy without overcomplications. No, it was not his smile at all.

It was his heart.

The Biggest of Human Illusions

CHAPTER 22

Control. The biggest of human illusions. Ever since we are self-aware, we are immersed in and absorbed by the fallacy of control. We are convinced that everything we do, everything we decide, everything we want, is based on our inherent ability to choose for ourselves--the gift of free will. Unlike animals, who act instinctively, we grow up convinced that our main difference from the animal world is that we can process information and come up with sound and logical choices, based on our decision-making capacity.

I sat in the empty lounge (after a carb-filled lunch, digestion takes first dibs on the blood supply and adds to the drowsiness of the drugs, so most of the patients spend the next hour or so in bed), conversing with the broken clock, trying my best not to think about anything negative, hoping that I would get to go home soon. Silence spread over the psychiatric floor like the plague, and other than the occasional keystroke from the nurse's station, everything else was mute. Trying to fill the quiet encouraged me to wonder if we truly had as much control as we thought we did. *Hear me out*, I told the clock. *I think I got something here.*

The decisions that we make consciously are based on logical reasoning, or so we think. But a lot of the time that reasoning is based on illogical behavior based on emotion. *Well, whaddaya mean, Jay?* the broken clock asked.

What I mean is that our decisions are highly influenced by chemical and emotional factors; the way we see the world at any point in time is due to the juices flowing in our head, and the way they make us feel. This is why we can be in the same place, experiencing the same thing, on two different occasions, and the experience could feel totally different if we are in another frame of mind the second time. The way we also handle certain situations is also based, well… I don't need to repeat myself.

Every day we walk around convinced that we are the captain of the ship, and we steer that ship based on the wisdom and knowledge we have acquired throughout our lives. We feel confident that we are smart and mature enough to analyze and process whatever information gets thrown at us, then, with calculated precision, we can make a decision and take action to successfully deal with whatever has been sprung on us. So, when the storm comes, we are supposedly intelligent enough to choose the right direction in which to point the boat, and don't get me wrong, this is partially true, but not as true as we make it out to be.

And what led you to that conclusion?

A few things. First, I realized what anxiety really is. Anxiety is something coming your way, and you not having the confidence to believe that you can deal with it. Opposed to the instinctive confidence that I just mentioned, severe anxiety will paralyze you and not let you act accordingly. It will create an acute amount of fear that will only let you see what is in front of you through augmented lenses, making everything seem closer, bigger and stronger. This, of course, is only in your head most of the time, and your skewed perception of a situation stops you dead in your tracks. But it isn't real; it's just your mind. But then again, isn't everything real to you the product of your mind? Something else to ponder on.

Second, the fact that my outlook on the same exact world changed with one pill once again proves my point. Neither my circumstances, nor my problems, nor my past or my present changed at all from three days ago, when the load was so heavy and dire that I considered ending it all. Nothing changed, except my outlook and the way I feel. When things become less overwhelming and you stop feeling threatened, your views on them dramatically change. The way you see things is obviously chemically and emotionally charged, with just a hint of self-awareness sprinkled in, to hopefully guide you logically. Or what about when I was another person under the effects of drugs and alcohol? I became reckless and made choices that I would have never considered sober; I was a different person with a malfunctioning mind, a monster that had thoughts of its own, desires of its own, an agenda of its own. When I would wake up after being blacked out for a while I couldn't fathom how I did some of the things that I did. Even before, when chasing the high, my brain's chemical need motivated me to do what was necessary in order to get its fix. It didn't matter if I was sober and in a supposedly clear state of mind, perfectly able to make a sound decision. The need becomes greater, just like hunger for food and thirst for water. Your brain sends the signals and most of the time, you acquiesce.

Ok, so let's bring it a little closer to home. Take the following example into consideration: you fall "in love" with a girl, and that "love" makes you start seeing her as the gem she isn't, the most perfect human being on the planet, tailored by fate specifically for you; the soulmate that only comes once in a lifetime. Her flaws don't matter and are easily excused, her weaknesses and her lies are not even acknowledged, all the roadblocks and firewalls piling up in front of you are not even detected, and you do this because your brain is flooded with all the juices that will not let you see anything else but the colorful and misguided hope that we all hang on to from time to time. It's like being colorblind, if colors were the serious, potentially harmful flaws of the person you like. I honestly think that if you didn't get blinders over your eyes when you are attracted to someone, it is likely that the entire human race would've died out thousands of years ago.

So, let's say that you finally get what you want and she gives you a shot; you two end up together. Those chemicals that pushed you to go on the hunt, that drove you to do whatever was necessary to get her (the things you once thought unthinkable, about which you said: *I will never do that for a woman*), are now gone, since they are no longer needed. The hunt is over, the price was redeemed, the king gets to feast on his accomplishments, and eat, and rest, and play Call of Duty online until all his friends know who's boss, yes, the one who got the perfect girl and the highest score. But now she asks you why you don't look at her the same way anymore, why you don't go on those long walks with her any longer, or make love to her with the same intensity as before. A couple of years later she gets tired of the boredom that plagues the relationship, and she ends up chasing the excitement of another brain with fresh juices. You end up alone, and in the despair of your desolation you ask yourself how you were capable of neglecting her in so many ways, of being so lazy with so many things. You knew damn well she could find anyone else to love her, you know, with her being the most perfect human being on the planet and all.

Just kidding. It's the juices again.

So the questions beg: Who am I really? What is my true reality? When is it that I see the world for what it is? Is it when the curtains are pulled back by the depression and I can see the mess backstage, or is it when I walk through the peaceful flower gardens and the euphoric afternoons of a drug-induced sensation, or when the Effexor hits and I become energized and filled with a profound sense of ambition?

How many versions of me are there? Is my reality "the" reality, or is reality a figment of our imagination, something created from the inside out instead of the other way around, something esoterically personal and as unique as our fingerprints?

So where is it that circumstances, learning experiences, time and love fit into your equations? the clock asked.

I obviously don't have it all figured out yet, and I don't think that any of us ever will. What I do know is that there is a veil over our eyes, the illusion of control, and that illusion could possibly be dangerous. We need to understand our limitations and figure out how to get the flow of brain juices that will allow us to control our path just enough to make it positive. We need to become more aware of our instincts and our subconscious, and with practice, learn how to handle our emotions better, and most importantly, have a higher ratio of logical to emotional decision-making ability, which will give us a little more control than what we actually have.

Look at you, going on a rant. You sound like you really belong here now.

I guess the medication gives me a boost. Who knows if I would've had the same thoughts without it, and that again proves my point.

This is confusing.

And I am talking to a clock.

I am a faithful witness of all that has happened in here. For years.

That's true. So what's your input?

I think humans are simple creatures. You overcomplicate things. You rely too much on your minds; that is what you are taught to do. But let me tell you that throughout the years I have met amazing people with very poor-functioning minds. It isn't their minds that make them great, it's who they are inside.

I thought your mind is who YOU are inside? I questioned the clock's logic.

In part. Your mind is more the antenna that picks up the broadcast. Sometimes, if it's not pointed in the right direction, it can pick up a little bit of static noise, sometimes a lot. But that doesn't mean it isn't good programming.

That makes sense in an interesting kind of way. Thank you for the timely input.

Good pun. Nicely done.

I continued to sit, bathed in a pile of boredom, counting the minutes, trying to persuade the clock to tick a little faster. But it didn't budge; it was enjoying the conversation too much. Sometimes I should really learn to keep my mouth shut.

CHAPTER 23

I found myself once again sitting on the exam table in the crowded little room, wearing nothing more than the hideous green hospital gown and the tremors that crawled up my spine from the freezing temperature. I was surrounded by generic gray cabinets that were labeled and locked, containing everything from gauzes, cotton swabs and syringes, tongue depressors, isopropyl alcohol and rubber gloves. The exam table was slanted in a corner and a small desk with a computer stood next to it. There were posters on the wall advertising certain drugs, and one with ten cartoon faces, each one agonizing a little more than the last, from left to right. On the top was the question: *In How Much Pain Are You?* For a second I wondered if the poster referred only to physical pain, or if there was another chart for emotional distress as well. There was a plastic brain on the desk that split down the middle, so your doctor could pinpoint exactly what part of your head was fried, and a couple of notepads branded with prescription drug names, which promised to help "un-fry" some of that damage.

I sat there, waiting, trembling, my body working tirelessly at keeping my core temperature intact.

A white coat barged in the room. On the left breast pocket were a couple of pens and the name *Dr. Murray* embroidered in italics. He jumped on the computer without saying a word, displaying a sense of urgency that made me realize he was in the volume business. He shook the computer mouse vigorously to get the monitor to wake up. "Let's see what we got here," he mumbled. He was a lanky middle-aged man with a full set of white hair, a little too white to be considered distinguished. He wore round, thin glasses-- much like the ones Steve Jobs used to wear-- and he exuded a hint of condescension that was difficult not to smell in such a small space.

He looked at the top of the chart he was carrying and read my full name. "Jay Rodriguez. Let's take a look at your blood test results." He clicked a few keys and the computer spat out what looked to be a detailed lab report. Dr. Murray rolled the wheel on top of the mouse with his index finger as he scanned in silence. "Good, good, Vitamin B a little low, good, oh..."

"Oh?" I asked, worried.

"Your liver enzymes are quite elevated," he said, not with concern, but more like a high school science teacher lecturing a ninth-grade class. "Normal to happen to people who abuse drugs and alcohol, but still worrisome. Your liver is most likely fatty, which is a reversible condition, but if it turns fibrotic it will most likely turn cirrhotic over time, and there is no turning back from that."

"How bad is this cirrhotic liver condition?" I asked with a little apprehension.

"It's as bad as it gets," he said nonchalantly, as a sigh escaped his lungs and he looked at the Rolex that clung from his wrist, a gentle reminder that I was beginning to waste his time by asking silly questions. "Your liver will gradually cease to perform the important functions that it's responsible for, and you will end up with some nasty side effects that will eventually kill you, and not in the most pleasant of ways." I could almost see a smile beginning to form on one side of his mouth, the thought of an addict dying in agony like the worthless piece of shit he was bringing joy to his heart. "Like, for example, ascites, which is when your legs and then your belly fill up with fluid, and it must be extracted through a tube in the side of your belly, a fun little procedure called paracentesis. A lot of people have to get fluid drawn out on a weekly basis. There is also portal hypertension, that results from high blood pressure in the portal vein and leads to esophageal varices that will burst from time to time. The first couple of times, if you make it to the hospital fast enough they might be able to save you, but every time it happens your chances of surviving diminish significantly. Oh, and I almost forgot about hepatic encephalopathy..." His eyes were now gleaming with satisfaction, the fact that he wasn't teaching me, but sentencing me for all my sins a great source of amusement for him. "... which is when all the toxins that your body can no longer remove go up to your brain and, well, let's just say it's not much fun after that."

The palms of my hands were now drenched in sweat and my heart was beating rapidly. He turned his attention back to the data on the computer. "Drugs in your system: benzos, cocaine, opiates." He shook his head, a fictional display of disappointment. "Not good Jay, not good at all." He put the stethoscope he had around his neck to his ears and placed the diaphragm on my back. "Take a deep breath... good, and again... one more time. Man, your heart is going! Thank you. Lie down please." He pushed my stomach down in several places with the tips of his fingers, then brought my socks down a bit and checked my legs for swelling.

"I can't believe it. Unbelievable... just unbelievable," he whispered as he checked me out. I don't know if he wanted me to hear him, or talking to himself out loud was just part of his cheeky personality. Either way, I became somewhat unsettled.

"Everything ok?"

He chuckled sarcastically. "Everything ok, yeah no. The Democrats with their shenanigans are making sure of that." There were many things that I could have expected to come out of his mouth in that moment - *I'm noticing some troubling signs, this doesn't feel just right, we might have to do a few more tests* – but what actually heard I would have never, in a million years, have guessed. I was so confused by his answer that I started to think that the hepatic encephalopathy was already making me lose my mind.

"Stupid tax reforms," he scoffed. "What are they thinking? Soon enough no one will be able to own a business in this country anymore! And for what? Welfare? Taking care of the ones that don't contribute?" he chortled. "They are going to be the death of us... the death of us."

I didn't know whether to nod or say something, so I stayed quiet. I felt like I was in one of those hidden camera shows, where they put you in a seemingly normal situation – maybe at job interview, or sitting at the cafeteria in the mall, or even at a park bench – and some strangers around you start acting erratically toward you or toward each other, and then your reaction to the whole thing becomes the punchline to the joke. I even thought that this could be just a test that I was being put through to determine my level of sanity, and behind a see-through mirror somewhere was Dr. Patel, scribbling notes on my chart. "I'm telling you," he continued. "They get to Congress and they start fucking everything up, and no one does anything about it. No one!" He was visibly upset now, all semblance of a smile gone, his forehead furrowed. "It's the Republicans' fault too, you know. We let them get away with too much, all the time... you can sit back up." He opened one of the drawers and grabbed a tongue depressor. "Open for me, say AAHHH."

"AAHHH..."

"And you know what's worse, the media, oh the media... trying to convince everyone that this reform is good for the economy." He shrugged. "Such bullshit... ok you can close now."

He jumped back on the desk and pounded away on the keyboard for a few more seconds, inputting the information he had collected into the database. "I'm prescribing you a Vitamin B tablet in the morning. That's all." The chart made an audible SNAP as it closed shut and Dr. Murray walked out of the room, almost as if he had just remembered that he was late for an appointment.

I sat there for a minute, green gown opened in the back and barely clinging to my shoulders, socks halfway down my feet, dumbfounded. Out of all the interactions I had after arriving here, this was by far the strangest. At first, I thought that someone would come for me, or at least someone would have to; I was in such a mental fog that I didn't even know where to go. I eventually collected myself and walked out of the little room, and my disorientation now turned into a rush of urgency. I needed to get back to my room quickly, to write a reminder to check for symptoms of liver problems on the Internet, and of course, to study up on tax reform.

CHAPTER 24

The panel consisted of two registered nurses, a social worker, a mental health counselor and her assistant, who had a laptop in front of her, a distinctive *clickity clickity* sound coming from the keys as she passionately typed with her long nails. They had joined two rectangular tables together and were sitting on one side, much like the judges would on those talent competitions on TV. On one end of the extended table was a stack of manila folders, each with enough paper inside to be considered the manuscript of a novel, and probably with material good enough to make it to the top of the bestsellers list. I sat in a lonely chair in front of the table, about five feet back, the distance between me and them making me feel like I was facing a jury of my peers, who would decide whether I lived or died. The conference room had an unusually high ceiling, with intricate trimmings that surrounded it like a crown, leading me to believe that this was one of the ballrooms back in the fifties, when I'd heard that the building was still an upscale hotel. Who knows how many people had their first dance here as husband and wife, their families and friends surrounding them as they embraced each other in a well-rehearsed waltz, a live band playing flawlessly while cigarette smoke rose and hovered over everyone, waiters in black and white catered to the guests and red lipstick left kisses on table napkins. All that was left from those times were ghostly memories, and a reception hall that was dark, dusty and barely used, with nothing now but the noise of the keyboard resonating and echoing against the walls. There was a window with a thick wooden frame parallel to my chair, the midday sun coming through it with strength, shining on me like a spotlight. The rest of the room was empty and eerie, and sitting this far back I could only see the silhouettes of the people in front of me, adding to the grimness of the entire thing.

A heavyset woman who was sitting in the middle of the tables whispered to the person over to her left, and that person whispered to the person at the end. One manila folder was passed down and opened. She briefly scanned the information inside. Other than the *clickity clack* of the keyboard and its echo, there was an absolute silence that penetrated skin and bone, uncomfortable and dry, rough to the touch. Someone discreetly coughed and scratched their throat.

Clickity Clack… Clickity Clack…

"Jay Rodriguez," the woman read the name on the chart out loud. Her deep voice bounced off the walls and the walls almost repeated my name perfectly. *This is what it feels like to be sentenced to death,* I thought.

Clickity Clack…

"My name is Ruth Vargas and I have been assigned to be your mental health counselor. The reason for this meeting is to come up with a plan of action in regard to helping you incorporate back into society when you leave us. It is important to have a plan that you can follow and work toward. Studies suggest that individuals with a strong plan and goal are more likely to succeed. My team is responsible for ensuring that first, you will be ready to leave us safely, that you will have a concrete plan to execute and, most importantly, that you will have a strong support group to be there when you need them. Do you understand?"

I nodded without saying a word.

"Can you tell us the reason you are here, Jay?" she asked. *There they go again with the redundant questions.* For a second I became angry, not understanding why they had to make me repeat myself over and over about something they already knew. *Don't you have everything you need right in front of you, lady?* I almost let my mouth slip, but then I concluded that any defiance of the establishment could only result in an extended and very unwelcome stay.

I took a deep breath, trying hard for my irritation not to be conspicuous. "Well…" the walls also seemed attracted to my voice. It was kind of weird to hear my own voice regurgitating what I was saying; it was as if my conscience was now outside of my body, and it repeated everything I said, in a disparaging attempt at drilling the regret deeper inside me. "I have been experiencing severe depression and suicidal thoughts. I didn't really know where else to turn so I came here."

"You have also been using hardcore drugs," said a rigid voice from behind the stack of manila folders. I couldn't even see the shadow of the person that spoke, but his condemning tone and the condescending way that his words rolled off his tongue told me more about him than his physical appearance ever could. "Are you an addict?"

I bowed my head and remained quiet. I had never admitted to anyone that I was a full-blown addict. I had never admitted it to myself. I took another deep breath. "Yes…" The walls echoed. The keyboard stopped.

"How often do you use cocaine?" the voice continued the interrogation.

"I don't know," I replied. "I only use when I am on other drugs."

"Which drugs, specifically?"

"Xanax," I answered. "It drives me to it."

Clickity Clack.

"Do you have housing, Jay?" Ruth asked, her voice now softer and higher pitched, as if trying to make up for the rudeness of the one before it.

"I live with my parents at the moment," I said, with honest

embarrassment.

"Do you work?" the person behind the folders asked.

"I don't have a steady job, no." More shame spumed inside me. I wanted so badly to tell these people that I was not a bad person, that I had good intentions and that I could handle myself fairly well, that with the right outlook I could do good things and be a contributing member of society. But the truth was that the more I spoke, the less of a leg I had to stand on.

The keyboard continued clacking and the silhouettes started talking amongst themselves in hushed tones. They deliberated for a while and then the silence hovered above us again, like the cigarette smoke did back in the day. Ruth spoke.

"How can we help you, Jay? What do you want to accomplish?"

Those questions struck me like a lightning bolt and kept me perplexed for a moment. I had come to this place in a state of despair, in a feeble attempt at saving me from myself. I had never, however, thought long term. I didn't think I *had* long term. What did I want to accomplish? In what direction did I really want to take my life?

"Well..." I cleared my throat. "I do want to get sober, have a more positive outlook on the future, and hopefully continue receiving therapeutic help. I like what I have accomplished with Dr. Patel." There were a few more seconds of silence. The voice that bounced off the walls and repeated my words sounded weak and insecure; it wasn't trying to judge me anymore; it had joined me in doubt, and it attempted to comfort me.

"Thank you, that's all we need today," another voice said.

I was more shocked than pleased by the abrupt end to the meeting. Had I said something wrong? Did I fail the test? I stood up without saying a word, leaving the silence undisturbed. I looked up and there they were again, the dust specks, dancing right in front of me, sharing the spotlight. I glanced at the dark faces, which were now again whispering amongst each other. The manila folder traveled back to the pile. The *clickity clack* of the keyboard continued and my steps echoed as I walked out of the light, leaving an empty chair behind.

As I made my way back to the third floor accompanied by a nurse, I began to feel unwell. My head was throbbing and my stomach weak. The walls looked fuzzy and my feet trembled. I started to sweat profusely. *Withdrawals*, I thought. *Just what I need.* I barely made it the room on my own two feet. Bob walked in after a long reading session, and as soon as he put eyes on me he grew concerned. "Jay, are you ok?"

"Bob..." I said, shaking, "what would you like to accomplish? What would...you...li..." Everything went black.

What happened next I can only remember in bits and pieces. I opened my eyes momentarily and saw Tony, felt pressure on my left arm and looked at it. There was a blood pressure cuff wrapped around it. "Hang in there, my brother." Tony's distant voice made me feel less alone. Then black. Then I heard Bob reading the bible close by. John 3:16, *For God so loved the world that he gave his one and only Son, that whoever believes in him shall not perish but have eternal life.* Her favorite scripture. Then black. I felt someone stroking my hair softly. I saw Callie. It felt nice. I wanted to ask her how she had managed to sneak into my room without getting in trouble, and most importantly, thank her for it, but I didn't have the strength. Then black. I went back into the room where I had previously been that morning. Five shadows sat in front of me on the opposite side of the table, as the *clickity clack* of the keyboard got louder and louder. "What do you want to accomplish?" a voice asked. "What do you want to accomplish!" it now yelled. *Clickity Clack, Clickity Clack, Clickity Clack* The light of the sun shining through the window became gradually brighter and brighter, so bright that I could no longer keep my eyes open, and brighter and brighter; I was engulfed in a wave of blinding radiance that wrapped around me and hugged me so tight I could barely move. *Clickity Clack Clickity Clack, CLICKITY CLACK CLICKITY CLACK*

I screamed at the top of my lungs, my voice becoming the highest-pitched noise I had ever heard, so high that it morphed into a frequency that human ears could not detect. The sun had turned into a light bulb, hanging from a wire in the middle of the ceiling of the little examination room, the acute noise expelled by my lungs making it burst and shatter. Then black.

I awoke and sat up on the bed, breathing heavily. The sheets were drenched in sweat and so was I. It was nighttime, and the lights of the room were off. "Welcome back," I heard Bob's voice to the right. He looked at me as if he had been patiently awaiting my arrival for a while and knew that it could be any moment now, so he was not at all surprised.

"How long?" I asked.

"Almost twenty-four hours," he replied. "They say benzo withdrawals can get pretty gnarly. You will survive though."

"My parents, did they come? Did they visit?" I was concerned they were worried.

"They did, and Tara kept them entertained for a while," he said. "I think your dad gave her permission to ask for your hand in matrimony," he laughed. "But they did see you for a few minutes. Tony worked it out."

I lay back down. My head was still pounding but the nausea was gone. "They are giving you a pretty high dosage of Librium," Bob said. "They are going to have to taper you off that gradually, but that should handle the withdrawal symptoms."

"Bob... thank you," I said gratefully.

"It's not like I had a choice!" he laughed. Then he looked at me with tender eyes.

"You're welcome. Get some rest, kid, and let's see if you can accomplish sitting at the breakfast table tomorrow."

Sitting at the breakfast table. The thought of being able to get out of bed and just sit at a table brought me an incredible sense of comfort and peace. I felt like in the miniscule amount of time I had been here I had grown my family by several members, and there was nothing I wanted more than to spend some time with them while breaking bread. And then it hit me. That was what I wanted; that's all that I ever wanted.

Peace.

CHAPTER 25

William is disoriented, adrift, lost in his own confusion, not knowing where he is, or why. The world is a hazy blur that does not allow him to clearly see what is in front of him; everything seems lethargic. He looks around the room, exploring the faces around him, his eyes dry and empty, bewildered with the struggle of not remembering much.

"Hi William," a woman speaks delicately. "Welcome to our process group. I heard you just got in. How do you feel?"

He is an old man reaching seventy, with bottle-bottom glasses and a Hawaiian shirt that allows the top of his chest hairs to shine through, gray and lanky, spitting out of his pores in all different directions, like they were exploding out of his bust. His white mustache hangs over his top lip and trembles when he speaks, giving it life of its own. He sits with hands resting on his lap and back straight on the chair. It is hard to see his brown, haggard eyes through the thick lenses, but it's obvious that he's afraid.

"I'm... ok... I guess..." The mustache quivers. "Could you tell me where I'm at?" he asks with timidity.

"Of course, William," she says with an earnest smile. "You are in Memorial Hospital, recovering after your first round of ECT. Do you remember?"

He squints his eyes and his forehead forges new lines, a committed attempt at spitting out a memory, but everything remains clouded and scattered. Gradually, however, as his focus is regained and the fog starts to clear, broken scenes begin to emerge. "Billy! Get your ass over here and jump in the tub!" his mother yells as he chases his little brother around the pasture. The farm is big and full of animals: horses, cows, pigs, hens. It has been passed down from generation to generation, and it is the staple and foundation of the family's pride. It clothed and fed every single one of Billy's relatives, without exception, and through the hard times — the tornadoes and the droughts and the downy mildew — they were able to make it to the other side and keep the farm alive. But Billy knows his father never wanted to follow in everyone else's footsteps — he looked up at the city life like the religious look up at heaven; the one place that will truly give you everything you need to be happy, forever - and having to do so made him bitter as the years went by. He walks in the house with intimidating authority, wearing his cowboy hat and double stitched leather boots.

"Billy, Johnny, go to your room, now!" Mother yells at the top of her lungs as the father stumbles in, having trouble putting one foot in front of the other. She knows what is about to happen; it's a movie that has played over and over too often lately. But her priorities are her boys, who have already seen too much, unfortunately. By now they both know the protocol: go to the room, turn the light off and sit on the floor in the farthest corner from the door. From the room, Billy can hear the sound of a thick leather belt that flattens his mother's back with blunt force. She tries to hold her cries as he fiercely beats her, but it's too much to bear. She howls in relentless agony, and Billy puts his hands over his little brother's ears, who quietly sobs. There is a single tear that tickles his left cheek as it runs down his face with patience, but Billy ignores the desire to wipe it off, in order to keep his little brother in the silence. The sound of leather against skin stops and it's replaced with boot steps that get louder as they approach the bedroom door...

Things get clouded again.

He looks out in the distance at a Pacific Ocean that salutes him with a dance of waves that crash carelessly on the shore. Seagulls chirp over his head as he runs toward the water with surfboard in hand.

There is a girl, a wood fire, bongo music and flower tiaras. There is a kiss, unforgettable as a night sky, full of music and stars, sweet like fresh honey that slowly drips from the comb. He is thousands of miles away from the farm, his mother long gone in the bittersweet rapture of an early death, which Billy convinced himself was God's way of giving her the peace she deserved. His brother had moved away long before, when his father found him making out with one of the boys from town, and beat him so badly he had broken two ribs. But big city life was a monster that the young man was not prepared to confront – he had always been under his mother's wing and the protection of his brother – and a year later he was putting a bullet hole in the back of his skull. Billy didn't go to the funeral; he wanted to remember his little brother as he always had, happy and cheerful, running barefoot around the pasture, while his big brother stayed close behind. His father was still alive, angry and drunk, having no other choice but to keep up with a farm that gave him more headaches than crops. Billy knew that it was the perfect punishment for the man, and fervently prayed and begged God to keep him alive for a few more decades.

The sunlight now dims and changes colors: blue, red, green. They move and fluctuate on stage as Billy makes a guitar sing and people bounce in motion in the darkness of the pit. A man with long blonde hair and black sleeveless shirt passionately grabs the mic and begins to sing. A girl on top of a guy's shoulders sticks out her tongue and lifts her shirt, exposing her naked breasts. Heads move up and down to the rhythm of the music like popcorn in the microwave, and the drum solo extends the song for an extra three very welcome minutes. The music fades and the colors blur; there is now a belt strapped around Billy's upper arm, producing a thick, throbbing vein that welcomes a needle. Then, another honey-like kiss.

He looks up and a beautiful blonde dressed all in white is beaming with a smile while she holds his hands. Her lips move and although there is no sound, he knows that a promise is being made. He looks down and, to his surprise, there is a small baby sleeping carelessly in his arms, a flower tiara adorning her tiny head and a pink pacifier dancing delicately in her mouth. Another needle goes in the arm, another sweet kiss. There is now a little girl, blonde as the sun itself, blue-eyed like the Pacific Ocean that gifted her to him, doing cartwheels around him with the type of energy that only a child is privileged to have. She stops momentarily and blows him a kiss, then runs to a corner of the room. She lifts both of her arms above her head, lifts one heel and arches her back forward, much like an Olympic gymnast. Hands and feet take turns in bouncing off the carpet, and when she lands on the other side of the room, she is now a vibrant, beautiful pre-teen, eyes bluer than ever, hair brighter and longer, almost as if California itself had given birth to her.

Another needle, another kiss.

A middle-aged woman, haggard and much older looking than what she should be, shoves him furiously, bathed in anxious sweat, anger and apathy, yet with enough strength to make him fall against the wall. She is yelling, her breath warm against his face, but he cannot comprehend what she says. He's angry, but he doesn't know why; it is just an unexplained rage, one that blinds whatever common sense he has left. His fist goes up and strikes. Everything goes dark. There are now metal bars all around him; they clink as a baton takes roll call. They feel colder than ice, harder than steel. There is not another needle, much less another kiss.

A gate opens and a guard watches his steps as he crosses the line back to freedom. He now sits on a dirty mattress, the only piece of furniture that the small room that he is in contains. There she is, the little girl twirling and dancing all over the place; the same tiara adorning her head, a pink tutu around her waist. She is happy and innocent and immaculate, perfect as he's always seen her, but he knows it is all a mirage, brought on by a colossal sense of regret. His eyes become damp with painful tears. The walls of the room start to retreat and split open, almost like they were part of a puzzle that someone is pulling apart. A nurse walks in and hands him a pill. She is wearing all white, and it makes him cringe, the memory of the last woman he saw in white vividly appearing. He swallows the pill and shuts his eyelids, begging for the absence of pain, his clamor going unheard.

A drop of water falls on his head, then another, and another. It begins to precipitate and he makes use of the black umbrella in his right hand. He stands on freshly cut, green grass that sparkles as the raindrops cover it and make it reflect light, almost like diamonds. There is a tombstone a few feet away, but he is not close enough to read what is engraved on it. He walks over with mild curiosity, his eyes widening and his legs weakening, making him fall to his knees in complete surrender as he reads the name. He is holding roses in his left hand, which he gently puts down and waters with his own tears. The rain continues to fall, a little harder this time, the sound deafening to his ears. He drops the umbrella and lets the water flood him, hoping that if he stays long enough he will be able to drown in it. He looks down at his forearm, but this time there is no needle, but a razor blade instead. Blood paints the scene red and it pulsates to the rhythm of the sirens. There is a hospital bed, plastic tubes, transfusions and pulse monitors, a window with no view and a room with no visitors.

A nurse walks in and hands him another pill. As he begins to take it, the bed starts to retract and morph into an office chair, reminding him of those transformer robots from the movies he used to love. A doctor sits on a desk in front of him, giving the final touches to a script. Another empty room, filled only with the twirls of a happy little girl - yellow sun and blue sky - who refuses to leave. Nauseous, tired and defeated from all the pain, he grabs her by the hair and holds her head back, her neck extending to an abnormal length, her eyes changing from content to surprise to panic, while he shoves the entire contents of the pill bottle in her mouth. He screams in agony as he holds her lips shut and the little girl tries miserably to regurgitate, her chest bouncing up violently, almost like someone was punching her from inside. She begins turning blue, her struggle dissipates; the child ceases to breathe. Another fade to black, another ambulance ride.

He raises his eyes to find himself back in the present, between a young woman and a few patients in a circle of chairs. The memories were bright, but he feels no pain, there is no emotion, there is nothing there. "William…" the young voice asks again. "Do you remember?"
Electroconvulsive therapy, better known as ECT, is a procedure

where electrical currents are passed through the brain, intentionally provoking seizures. It has been proven to help alter brain chemistry, which can reverse the symptoms of certain mental illnesses, including severe depression. One of the side effects, however, can be memory loss.

William speaks from the back of his white mustache. "Yes... I remember."

Her smile, more intoxicating than the alcohol in my veins.

CHAPTER 26

"Tell me about her."

"Do I have to?"

"I think it would help."

"It's a little tough to talk about. Still raw."

"No one said it would be easy."

"I know..."

"Go on, whenever you are ready."

"I saw her for the first time at a church gathering I attended with my parents. The congregation had reserved a gazebo at a park for their regular monthly social. Most of the members collaborated with food and drinks, and by the time we arrived, there already was a colorful array of delicious entrees from which to choose: white and brown rice, black beans, pork, barbecued chicken and fried plantains. There was also deviled eggs and sugar ham and a *pico de gallo* that promised to turn your mouth into a *fiesta*. In a corner, an iPod plugged to a speaker played family-friendly tunes. Little kids ran around chasing each other with astonishing energy. The adults gathered at the food table and picked out their choices buffet style, then sat and ate while catching up with friends. There was a buzz of chatter that rose from the benches like smoke, indistinct voices talking at once, with an audible laugh taking over from time to time, a symphony of good vibes and comradery that I hated to admit was somewhat contagious.

"The park had more than a dozen gazebos, and on a beautiful summer day almost all of them would be filled with families and acquaintances - celebrating birthdays, baby showers, anniversaries, having dance parties, cooking on the grills or simply enjoying the weather - and this was one of those days. The sun had risen that morning with glaring ambition, painting a bright blue sky that the sea reflected immaculately. A breeze swept in and cooled the day, and more than a stimulating caress of fresh air, it made you feel alive as you took a deep breath, your lungs expanding with a batch of oxygen that smelled slightly different; pure and filtered by nature itself. Where the park ended, a beach began, and our gazebo was strategically positioned to have a perfect view of the horizon and, later that afternoon, of a sunset that would take place front and center - a stroke of bright yellow morphing into different hues of pinks and red, right before being swallowed by the great abyss - to the delight of all the spectators. The congregation always reserved that special spot months in advance, wanting all the ones present to marvel at God's creation.

"My parents had begged me for weeks to join them, in an attempt at getting me out of the house, away from my habits and surrounded by people of God, who could hopefully encourage me, motivate me and help me straighten out. It was a long shot, but worth a try. They had left the paper invite at the dinner table every night – a full page printout with a generic picture of a sunset that looked like it had been drawn by a child, and right underneath it the words JOIN US FOR A DAY IN THE PARK, WITH GREAT FOOD AND SPIRITUAL ASSOCIATON, followed by the address, gazebo number and the time the party would begin - a gentle, yet persistent reminder that they wanted me there. I agreed to go so I could get them off my back, but I never promised to do it sober. By the time we got there I already had three shots of vodka in my belly, and the flask in my pocket would soon add more to that number. I went straight to the buffet line and served myself a small portion of beans and pork. I could never drink on an empty stomach--it would make me nauseous and uncomfortable--so I always supplemented my alcohol with some solid food, but not enough to fill me up. I dragged a chair to one corner of the gazebo and sat facing the water, opposite of everyone else. I had hoped that I would go unnoticed, a lonely ghost who would eat some of the food and stay out of everyone's way, but I knew that would be a stretch for this bunch. Some of them came to say hello, with hypocritical smiles that proved they weren't doing it because they wanted to or because they cared, but simply because they thought they had to. They asked how I was doing with high-pitched voices and elongated words, the same way they would talk to a very young child, or a very old man. To them I was more like a cancer patient who didn't know he was dying, but they did, and they treated me with the pity they would treat someone that most likely wouldn't make it past the night. Then there were those faces that looked at me from a distance with disdain, patronizing me, thinking that my behavior was rude and petty, offended by my mere presence – this was a gathering of godly people, of spiritual uplifting, not an AA meeting - but I didn't care. I was drunk and I wanted to get drunker on the view and nothing else.

"As I looked out in the distance while bringing a fork toward my mouth, walking on the sand, a shape caught my attention. I squinted my eyes to block some of the glare and better focus on the person that I was seeing. She had long, straight, light brown hair and pearl-white skin, slightly reddened by the sun. She wore a flower dress that went up right above her knees, and she held her sandals in her hand, letting the sand play between her toes as she walked. She looked at the water as if she was looking at her old home, the one she was born and raised on. She was picking small shells off the sand, and her eyes marveled at each one, no matter how small or broken. To her, every single one was a universe, a story of a trip far into the heart of the ocean, a journey against the odds, one that culminated ashore. The wind would lift her hair and make it dance in the air, a wave that changed directions in the blink of an eye - sometimes extending straight behind her, parallel to the horizon, other times pushing it right in her face, like a playful toddler - but she didn't seem to care. She wasn't just another person who walked around the beach enjoying the landscape; no, she herself was part of it.

The very instant my eyes made contact with that woman, the world lost revolutions and the engine that kept it going slowed down and went silent. I could no longer hear the music in the background, or the buzzing of several conversations happening at once, or the chirps of the seagulls that flew by trying to scavenge, or the crash of the waves dying in the shore. The children were stopped in motion like wax statues, as if they had been frozen in time. A ball hung in the air, and the leaves that fell from the trees were suspended as well. My heart started beating faster when I noticed she was walking toward me, and at first I thought that I made my fascination for her too obvious. Maybe she had caught a glimpse of my interest and she had also become curious and wanted to engage. Maybe she had felt the same fascination for seeing one's future painted on the canvas of someone else's eyes, and she wanted to see what it felt like to create a special moment, where two complete strangers learn what love at first sight feels like. Maybe it was the beginning of a love story like no other. No, what was I thinking? I was being ridiculous. Yet she still walked this way. Closer... and closer. My heart now pounded as if I was running a marathon, and my already dilated pupils gave a slight haze to my vision. What should I do? What would I say? Could she be able to smell the alcohol in my breath? Did I have gum somewhere?

"Closer... and closer...

"With every step she took, she became more beautiful. God, I had underestimated her beauty.

"Closer... and closer....

"I could now barely contain myself. My hands were sweaty and my left leg bounced up and down uncontrollably. She was only a few feet away. I adopted a better posture and took a deep breath, preparing to engage in a (I hoped) pleasant and paradigm changing conversation.

"Closer...

"She walked right past me. I doubt that she even noticed that I was sitting there.

"*Of course*, I chuckled. I turned back in my chair and saw her walking toward a handsome young man who stood taller than most and who had the jawline of a model on one of those black and white fragrance commercials, the ones that always end up with someone whispering an Italian name. She came from behind and put her hands over his eyes. He smiled, not having to guess who it was. He turned with a gracious swiftness and grabbed her by her waist, picking her up from her feet and swinging her in the air. Then he slowly lowered her toward him and gave her a tender kiss on the lips.

"I smirked at my naivety in thinking that a girl like that would even notice me, let alone not be taken by some ex-high school quarterback, Mr. *I-get-who-I-want-when-I-want-it*. She was the kind of girl the square jaws of the world would get first dibs on, and the rest of us would have to continue dreaming, hopelessly. I turned back around and continued looking out at the water, as the world slowly picked up speed and resumed its activities at full volume. The kids unfroze and kept chasing each other, the ball fell and bounced off the ground, the leaves found comfortable rest on the grass. The music played and the people talked. Everyone had a good time.

"After sitting in my own filth for a while, I remembered the flask in my pocket and knew it was the perfect time to kick things up a notch. I walked across the gazebo and back toward the public restroom, which was about fifty feet away. I made eye contact with no one and everyone reciprocated the gesture, which I actually appreciated. I locked myself in the handicap stall, sat on the toilet and took the chrome container out of my pocket. I chugged about half of it, then did my usual swallowing exercise to avoid regurgitating. In about three and a half minutes the buzz took effect, and I could now go back and comfortably re-join the festivities. I got up and walked past the mirror on the sink, and for a moment I caught a glimpse of my reflection, a man I did not recognize, cynical and condescending, smug with another crushing victory under his belt. I paused, looked him straight in the eyes, gave him the middle finger and walked back to the seat I had previously occupied.

"The sun was beginning to set and now everyone behind me looked in the same direction. I could hear the voices talking about how marvelous the sunset was, how awe-inspiring. Someone asked how it was possible for a person to look at the sunset and not believe in God. *How in the heavens can someone see such natural beauty and not see a loving creator? How can someone visit the children's cancer ward and see one?* I thought. I was so buzzed by that time that I had to look back and make sure I hadn't said that out loud. I would have embarrassed my parents and then I would've had to hear it, not allowed to come back to next month's gathering. I saw her and jaw-man holding each other, seeing their future through the romantic appeal of the setting of the sun, the wonder of something that happens every day but never loses its beauty, something that always inspires and demands respect. I could see them thinking of all the sunsets they would see together throughout their happy lives, and my stomach jumped like a fetus does inside the amniotic sac, much to the mother's delight. I was forced to start doing my swallowing exercise again to avoid throwing up all over myself.

"I got annoyed with the whole thing and I asked my parents to take me home. When they noticed how toasted I was, they immediately obliged. I got home, went straight to bed and, when I closed my eyes, the first thing I saw was her face, her smile, her eyes. The breeze still played with her hair, and her pretty toes still had sand in them.

"That's it; that was the first time I saw her."

"When did you see her again?"

"A while later, maybe six months or so. I had been doing some electrical jobs with my dad when I was sober enough and needed some money to stop being so. Dad had mentioned that morning that we were going to go replace a faulty breaker at the Walkers, which meant absolutely nothing to me. I had no idea who the Walkers were. We knocked on the door early that morning. Having a busy day ahead of us, we wanted to get in and out quickly. The door slowly opened and a lightning bolt hit me dead center in the chest. There she was, in her unreal allure, in front of me, wearing a baby blue polka dot tea dress that made her look as bright as spring itself, her hair falling gently past her shoulders, covering part of her naked back. She was barefoot, her feet pure perfection, with small toes that all descended in size properly, like Matryoshka dolls; her nails were symmetrically flawless and pink, a small white flower living in the corner of her halluces.

"The Walker family had moved to the congregation about three years before. The head of the household, George Walker, was a hard-working father and husband who always made sure plenty of food was brought to the table. He was a respected businessman and elite member of the church. His family consisted of his wife, his daughter and the family poodle, Marcus. Weird name for a poodle, I always thought.

"When we got there that morning, Mr. Walker had to rush to go put out a hypothetical fire at one of his properties. He didn't leave without first instructing his daughter that she needed to let Mr. Rodriguez in the house so he could do the job and - he knew he didn't have to say it as he trusted her blindly - to please be a gracious host. My father was also a respected member of the congregation, and a very trustworthy man. Everyone wanted to ensure that they treated him well.

"She was as nice as she was pretty, her smile more intoxicating than the alcohol in my veins. She greeted us with freshly squeezed lemon juice and home baked cookies. She was humble and confident at the same time, and she ran the house well. You could tell she had been prepared from a very young age. I was shy and quiet at first, but I knew I would probably never have another chance like this again, where I would have all of her attention to myself. I began asking basic questions. *Where are you originally from? How do you like it here? What do you do in your free time?* Then I cracked a couple of silly jokes and she seemed to enjoy my sense of humor. I tried not to look or sound overly interested, but I never knew if I actually succeeded. Later, she would tell me how my eyes always told her everything. All I know is that when I left that house that day, she knew my name, and if I was ever to fall in love again it would be with her. In fact, I already had.

"I knew right then that I had no other choice but to go back to God, if I wanted a legitimate shot at being with her someday. My parents were thrilled when they saw me attending church on a regular basis and getting involved with the congregation again. It wasn't hard; it was all I had known growing up. With a little bit of time and effort, she started to notice the rise of my spiritual status and my reputation. It didn't take long for church members to welcome you back with open arms, as long as you were willing to do what you were supposed to, and you became a contributing member of the congregation. We became friends, and over time good friends, and then the type of friends that share secrets with each other that they don't with anyone else. The day that she was left heart-broken and desolated, I was the one that was there, and it was my shoulder that she cried on. Months passed by and I dedicated all the time I could to her, but it still took a while before she could look in my eyes and see me as more than a friend. When she finally did, and when *I* was the one that held her by the waist and attempted to toss her up in the air (and failed), I felt an incredible sense of accomplishment. The most perfect woman in the world was now mine."

"Did she know about your drinking problem?" Dr. Patel asked.

"She had gotten to know a lot of things about me, but the extent of my addiction I had managed to hide from her pretty well, as I did with everyone else. We had gone out a few times and I made sure not to get too fried, first so I wouldn't look ungodly, and second to not get sloppy. I could drink all I wanted when I got home, but when I was with her I made sure to hold off. Being with her brought me such peace and comfort that I really didn't feel like drinking when I was in her presence anyway. She was the most beautiful drug I had ever been addicted to."

"Thank you, Jay, thank you for sharing all that."

"It was tougher than I thought."

"How are you feeling now?"

"Lightheaded."

"You should lie down for a little while after we finish here today.

Make sure you continue taking the Librium along with the Effexor, and your withdrawal symptoms should hold back. Then we can start tapering you off the Librium. Benzodiazepine withdrawals can lead to seizures that can be deadly, so we want to make sure to take all precautions. Now that we have a better idea of how your body is responding we can act accordingly. Any thoughts of hurting yourself or others?"

"No."

"Hearing voices or seeing things that aren't there?"

"No."

"Good, very good. Any questions for me?"

"When can I go home?"

"You are here with voluntary status, Jay. You can go home whenever you choose. I would, however, advise that you stick around until you have at least detoxed, and we have you on the appropriate medication regimen."

"Can you tell me what my condition is?"

"I will give you an official diagnosis after we have the group session, with your parents."

"A group session... I don't know about that... I don't think I'm ready..."

"I think you are ready enough, and we need to do it in order to accurately diagnose you."

"If you say so... I guess I will have to soldier through it then."

"Great, thanks for always being a good team player. I know it can be hard sometimes. I think we are done here, Jay. Thank you... and wait! One more thing before you leave, and this one is off the record, but my curiosity begs… Do you still love her?"

CHAPTER 27

The lounge felt serene, a couple of card games in session and one or two inspired artists, keeping to themselves and their craft. A few zombies roamed the halls quietly, looking confused about the fact that there was no one else around. The nurse behind the counter had stopped typing on the keyboard for a while, letting random smiles escape her mouth as her face lit up with the glare of incoming text messages. I sat under the flickering lights, asking myself over and over the question Dr. Patel had previously asked me: *Do you still love her?* I wondered if my answer had been accurate, if I had been honest, if I truly knew.

I was feeling better. The withdrawals had diminished to a headache and a smidgen of nausea. I was fortunate that they hadn't lasted long; I later learned that some people experience some type of benzo-related withdrawal up to a year after quitting. All I knew was that I never wanted to go through that again. It was the closest I had ever felt to death, and the interesting part was that I didn't mind death; it was the severe physical discomfort mixed with mental torture that I could barely withstand. Bob had never left my side; every time I opened my eyes I could see him through the hazy blur, sitting there, like a soldier on watch, making sure to never leave his post. I had a lot to thank him for.

The low temperature in the lounge felt worse without bodies to absorb it, my joints aching and my hands turning a light shade of purple. I instinctively put them inside my pockets to try to regain some normal color and to ease the discomfort, grunting like a horse as I shuddered the chills away. I felt something in my right pocket that I didn't remember being there before, and instantly curious, I took it out to see what it was. I unfolded the small piece of college ruled notebook paper to find a Bible text written on it, from the letter of Paul to the Corinthians.

...Nor thieves, nor the greedy, nor drunkards, nor verbal abusers, nor swindlers, will inherit the Kingdom of God. And that is what some of you were. But you were washed, sanctified, you were justified, in the name of the Lord Jesus Christ and the spirit of our God.

Nicely played Bob, I smiled. *Nicely played.*

As I kept my eyes down while reading Bob's note, I felt the heaviness of eyes that rested upon me, making me feel uneasy, the same sensation that you get when you dream you are in a room full of people completely naked. I raised my head and looked around with discretion to see if I could spot the watcher. Nothing to my right except the unobstructed hall. Empty tables to my left and behind me, the broken clock. When I turned forward Maggie was standing there, in front of the table, looking at me. It felt like she had appeared out of nowhere, her eyes as wide as they went, her face stuck in its usual expression: mildly startled, like someone had jumped out of a bush in a semi-successful attempt at scaring her. "Hey... Maggie. Would you like to sit?" I asked her, slightly apprehensive.

She did not say a word, just stood there, motionless, for moments that felt like forever. Then she walked to my side of the table and sat on the chair to my right. She sat there, looking forward in excruciating silence, her hands tucked between her legs, not impervious to the cold. She was bathed in flawless black skin and wrapped in a shapely body that demanded attention even through her saggy gown. I could only imagine what an impact she would have on a man's eyes if she went through a slight makeover and wore a dress that highlighted her curves. She was a beautiful young woman. I could tell that she was nervous, her body fidgeting frequently and re-accommodating itself on the seat. I knew it had taken a great deal of courage to come sit by me, and I couldn't help to wonder what her reason for it was.

153

Jay Chirino

I remained next to her for a while in silent awkwardness. The broken clock enjoyed my misery; time felt like it was at a dead stop. The silence became agonizingly unbearable, almost palpable, the sort of cringe that makes you want to start making loud noises to get your mind focused on something else. On the one hand, I wanted to bounce off the chair and run; on the other, I didn't want to hurt Maggie's feelings. It was the first time I had seen her get close to someone and it felt like a big deal.

I endured until I could endure no more, then decided that it was time for me to go. I felt like things would just get more awkward if I extended my stay. Besides, maybe that was what she wanted; to make me feel uncomfortable enough so I would leave the empty lounge all to herself, and she could enjoy her solitude in peace. I began to stand up slowly, not to startle her. Halfway through I heard a voice I hadn't heard before, soft and sweet, yet filled with discernible pain. "You remind me of my brotha," Maggie said in a strong Haitian accent.

The process of standing up reversed into the process of sitting back down. Her voice was so low and timid, her accent so thick that I had a hard time understanding her. "Oh, what is his name?" I asked.

"Alexandre," she replied, still looking straight forward at the emptiness in front of her, far from making eye contact.

"That's very nice, Maggie," I said with an enthusiastic tone. "How often does Alexandre come see you?" *Boy, was that the wrong question to ask.*

Her big eyes shrank and filled with sadness as she looked down, distressed. "I don't see him no more. He dead now."

"Maggie..." I said. "I'm so sorry."

The walls of silence had now crumbled like a controlled implosion, and she continued to speak, delicately, painfully, like she was reliving the story for the very first time. "He lived in Haiti. I lived in Haiti. He... my younger brotha. Bad man came to hurt me, bad man my fatha, bad man hurt me for a long, long time. Bad man hurt me since

154

I was little girl." Tears emerged. "Alexandre find out and he get really mad, because he really, really love me, and he get so mad he go fight my fatha. But my fatha is very bad man, and he hit Alexandre in head with pipe, one time, and Alexandre brain stop working and he die. Month later." There were tears that rolled down her face, but they weren't sad tears. There was anger in her eyes, the quiet fury of feeling defenseless. Her lower lip trembled. For the first time, she turned her head and looked at me.

"Every time I see your eyes I see my Alexandre eyes, I see my little brotha... my little brotha love me very much and I love him very much, I see your eyes I see him." Then, in between tears and anger and grief, she smiled, and her smile was painfully tender, like the one of a child that got her innocence taken too soon. It was hard to grasp it at first; she didn't see me, she didn't see Jay. When she looked at me she was seeing the person who loved her most in the world, the person who gave his life for her, the person who saved her. I thought about how amazing this was and it moved me; it made me understand so much more about her. Her eyes clearly reflected years of unimaginable suffering and pain and loss, years of abuse that should not be mentioned, much less exist. She was a victim of the biggest crime that one can experience, the crime of someone taking your childhood away, a vile stroke of evil that lasts a lifetime. But there she was; one way or the other, she had made it through, and that was partly due to the little brother that she thought long gone, the little brother that she saw get killed with her own eyes, by her own father, the little brother that was now looking at her again, in the flesh.

"Maggie... it is an honor," I said, "to look at you and remind you of your Alexandre."

She blinked away a few tears and smiled, just slightly. "Thank you."

I thought about what I would do, if one day the big fan came to a stop and I woke up, a child again. There, walking through the door would be my grandfather, returning from that long trip they told me he went on. What would I do if I saw him there, in front of me, aviator glasses on his face and one of his cigarettes between his fingers, coming toward me with his usual swagger, the one he always had when he wasn't drunk. I wondered how I would react when he waved his hand, signaling me to get closer to him, opening his arms wide, preparing to eagerly embrace me, and squeeze me tight, and kiss me in the forehead, and hold me there for a while as his shoulder became humid with my tears. What would I do when he held my face and looked at me in the eyes, smiling, and I could tell that it was really him, that he had come back, and that the nightmare was over... what would I say?

Then I knew what I had to do in that moment. Maggie was sitting there, no longer fidgeting, her eyes calm as the waters of a lake. She looked like a different person, one who had just let go of an unimaginable and heavy burden, a darkness that had kept her quiet for many years. I leaned over and wrapped my arms around her, which at first surprised her and made her retract. Then I noticed the tension in her body dissipate; her face gently rested on my shoulder, and I felt her tender embrace as she began to sob. "There, there..." I whispered in her ear as I caressed her back, feeling her heart quicken. "It's ok. Everything is fine now, Maggie. Everything is fine. You're going to be ok. I'm here.

Alexandre is here."

CHAPTER 28

Callie stood in front of the big window wearing a gray Hollister hoodie, her - what I liked to call - fluffy pants and her Ugg booties. She had the hoodie up and I could only see half her face, from the nose down, giving her a keen resemblance to a character from an *Assassin's Creed* video game. She held a hot cup of coffee between her hands, trying to warm them up, while the steam danced up like a cobra and flushed her cheeks. It was still colder than normal in the psychiatric floor.

"I don't understand it, are they trying to cryogenically freeze us alive in here?" she complained as she vigorously shook her legs from side to side trying to get warm blood flowing to them. Her outfit made her look like she was a sorority girl nursing a Sunday hangover, carelessly young, an entire life ahead of her. It was only when you looked closer that you noticed her age in the creases of her skin and the sadness in her eyes. Even then she had managed to look beautiful; her legs amounted for a high percentage of her body, pretentiously long and thin, an effective weapon for emasculating the average man. If you woke next to her in the morning, her naked face being the first thing you saw, you ran the risk of never wanting to leave her.

"Don't stress about it; you're getting out of here anyway," I said. Her seventy-two-hour psychiatric hold had long expired and her dad had finally negotiated a deal with the Sunrise Center. Callie found me in the lounge after she heard the news, gave me a tight celebratory squeeze, then insisted in having coffee together by the window one last time. She had been disappointed though; the view hadn't changed much from before, but the playful birds were nowhere to be found.

"Do you think they are ok?" she said, her voice filled with concern. I was surprised at her honest worry for the little animals, insignificant as they were in the realm of things, microscopic in comparison to the dark reality that we both had lived. But she cared, she really cared, and it allowed me to see a side of Callie that maybe a select few had ever been able to see. I felt very grateful to have shared that moment with her.

"Callie, they are birds," I said, trying to ease her fear. "They fly to different places all the time. Today they are probably entertaining the grannies at the old folks' place down the street. I'm sure those old ladies get a kick out of the little buggers putting on a show for them." That made her smile. "I wish I was a bird," she said.

We stood there sipping on hot brew, absorbing as many sunrays as we could. The light and the coffee slightly raised our core temperatures, and Callie took off her hoodie, giving freedom to her soft blond hair, now traveling freely just past her shoulders. Today she looked better than she had before; she looked rested, tranquil, alive. The withdrawals hit her hard for the first couple of days, and seeing her close to normal showed me how much potential she truly had.

It was a perfect day outside, one of those days where even those indisposed to nature wouldn't mind going for a walk in the park, or maybe a bicycle ride, or a quick jog to get the heart pumping. But being on this side of the glass made us feel more caged than ever, the world out there getting farther from us as the day passed us by. "Are you excited?" I asked.

"Scared," she replied, looking down at her coffee.

"You are getting a new lease on life, Callie. This is it, you are going to go to Rehab and get hold of these issues once and for all. Then you will be really free."

"That is a wonderful thought," she said. "If only I believed it."

"Why Cal? Why don't you believe it?" I asked with a sprinkle of frustration.

"It's been so many years. I've failed so many times. I'm not a young woman anymore, Jay. It's been my entire life. I don't know what kind of person I am without the drugs," she said.

"A great one," I asserted. "All you have to do is believe in yourself, believe in your strength, the one you already carry with you." As I was saying those words, I realized that, although I was being completely honest, I wasn't really saying them to Callie. I looked through the glass and caught a glimpse of my reflection, and I knew that was the person who I was really talking to.

"Thank you, Jay," she said. "You always have a way of making me feel hopeful about things."

"I believe in you, Cal," I said with conviction. "I believe in us."
She raised her Styrofoam coffee cup in the air to make a toast. "To making better choices!"

"To making better choices!" I reciprocated, lightly touching my cup against hers.

We stood there for a while longer, watching the people below living their generic lives, mindlessly entering and exiting office doors, driving in and driving out, heads down, paying strict attention to their cellular screens, almost as if their lives depended on it. Callie and I began creating fictional stories about the characters that we spotted. She had a great imagination and could come up with detailed and extensive back stories. "See that guy right there, the bald one, with the Hawaiian shirt? That man is an undercover for sure. He dresses all causal and colorful to throw people off, but in reality, he works for the DEA. What nobody knows is that he also has a big coke problem, so all his busts are just a way of feeding his own habit..."
"You are good at this, Cal! I could do this all day," I laughed.

The sun got shy and the sky took a shade of gray. Dark clouds interfered with the blue and rain began to precipitate. Down below people ran for cover, some of them never breaking contact with their phones. A heavyset man slipped and fell on his butt, but no one noticed. He swiftly got up and kept going, as if nothing had occurred, the back of his shirt and black slacks soaked and dirty. "Ugh," Callie scuffed. "This just got real depressing. I might as well go pack up. It takes me a while." She gave me another hug, looked directly into my eyes and made me promise her that I would visit her after she got sober. We would go have coffee at a real coffee shop this time –no more muggy coffee and recyclable cups-- and we would people watch for hours while enjoying the taste of quality brew. We would also find time to pridefully talk about our accomplishments, and how addiction tried but failed to defeat us. We would reminisce about that stint that we had together in the psychiatric floor of Memorial Hospital, and we would cherish what we now had, aware of how much sacrifice it took.

A few hours later, as I saw the Prada luggage being carried out the double doors, I sincerely yearned for the time we could make all that a reality.

But we never did.

The next time I saw Callie was five years later, at her funeral. It was spring. The air felt crisp and sharp, and it bounced off the walls of buildings in New York City in an intermittent, yet invigorating flow. The church, decorated from top to bottom in white roses – which gave out a strong but pleasant fragrance – felt like a midway point between Earth and Heaven. There were more people there than there were benches; friends, families, colleagues, even some of the local media showed up. "She loved white everything," her mom said through some tears, but she looked numb, maybe hoping she was dreaming and was going to wake up at any time.

Her dad, on the other hand, was more visibly shaken than anyone else. His skin was pale and his eyes were dead. "I caused this…" he whispered. "I caused this…" he whispered again, a little louder this time. "I caused this… I caused this…" Every time he said it his voice grew more desperate. "I caused this, I caused this!" He fell to his knees weeping, both hands covering his face.

"Oh Jim!" his wife fell to the floor with him and wrapped her arms around him. "We have to be strong. That's what Callie would have wanted us to do."

After she left the hospital, Callie had been able to successfully complete her stay in Rehab and remained sober for the next four years. Her life took a dramatic turn for the better. She went back to school and got a degree as a dental assistant. Her dad worked his usual magic and got her a job at a dentist office through one of his old golf buddies. She moved out of her parents' house and now rented a small studio about thirty minutes south. She became hopeful and full of life, and without the toxins plaguing her body, she became twice as pretty as she was before.

Sometimes, however, beauty can attract suffering, and in Callie's case it came in the form of a hotshot lawyer by the name of Bill. She fell in love with Bill, his confident demeanor and his fast way of life almost immediately. He gave her the rush and filled the hole that the drugs had left behind. In her mind, they would be together until death did them part, and in between they would settle down and travel the world for a while. Then they would come home and have kids-- two to be exact: Billy Jr. and Lizzy. She always liked the name Lizzy.

But a year later Bill grew bored, as usual, and found a younger, firmer body with less mileage to satisfy his fleshly desires. Callie was devastated, but held it together for a few months. The day that she heard about Bill's engagement was the day that she lost all control.

She locked herself in her studio and became distant from everyone and everything. She stopped going to work, lost her job and her phone line, and nobody knew of her for three weeks. It was when her dad broke her front door down that he found her, on the living room floor, face down and naked, with a needle in her arm. Callie did not have enough money saved up to afford to go on her usual pill binge, so she had to resort to the cheaper, much deadlier option: heroin.

I made my way to the pearl-white casket with a small bouquet of roses in my hand. They were yellow instead of white, and I liked the fact that they stood out from the rest. I always liked to think that the moments that Callie and I spent together were deeply significant – as short as they were – in the sense that we saw each other without walls, vulnerable and defeated, yet we could see something special as well. I put the flowers on top of the casket and looked at her still body lying there, wearing a white dress and a small crown made of roses, her hands interlocked on her chest, and if you looked close enough, a painful smile on her face. She looked exactly like I remembered her, and how I had seen her in my dreams, when I thought about the coffee shop and the people watching, some day. I wish I had visited earlier.

I put my hand on top of hers as a couple of tears fell inside the casket. "You are free now, little bird. Go on now... go on and fly away."

CHAPTER 29

Dear Me,

I know, I also feel kind of silly writing you this letter, but Dr. Patel encouraged it and said it would probably help, so I trust her. Don't worry, you're not dying or anything; she's a different type of doctor. You will meet her someday out there in the future, and you will be really glad you did.

I know what you are currently going through. I haven't forgotten. Your life will be molded and shaped by some of the displeasing things that are happening in it right now. However, I have recently learned that this is not a bad thing. It will help you grow and it will help you learn, and it will someday, I hope, make you a better man. I know that you are afraid, and it's a fear you cannot explain. I know you think the world is bleak, and you are right to an extent. But I also know that deep inside there is a part of you that wants to believe in the beautiful and the romantic, in the colorful and sublime. I know that you want to explore, and learn, and see beauty where no one else can. I know you want to be someone significant, someone who matters. I know that you wish you could fly and see the world from above, without fear of falling, seeing every imperfection and every virtue in a universe full of hope. I know that there is greatness within you that you don't know exists and that you will doubt for many years, but it's there, and it will shine in all its glory one day, just at the right time. When and where, we both have yet to find out.

Unfortunately, time travel has not been invented yet, although it would be really cool if it was. There are a lot of people who would like to go back and fix the mistakes they made, but if you ask me, they would just repeat them all over again, maybe at a different time and a different place. This is not the purpose of this letter; I'm not here to fix you or tell you what to change. If I did, if I encouraged you to be someone else, there would be a much different man writing you this letter, and as much as I dislike who I am sometimes, I've also realized that I am pleased with who I'm not. Like I said, there is greatness in you, and I can't wait to see when it finally shows up.

I wish I could tell you that things are going to get a lot better, that you are going to skip through life like you sometimes do when the bell rings and it is time to go home from school. I wish I could say that some of your wildest dreams have come true, and that you are a man of good, the pride of everyone in the family. I wish I could tell you that people look up to you and see you as the man you really are, but if I did I would not be telling you the truth. I don't mean to make you sad or discourage you, but if there is one thing that I have learned lately it is that, in order to get better, I have to be completely honest with myself, and that, of course, also means being completely honest with you. You will face challenges, serious ones, that will test you like you never thought you would be tested and will bring you to the brink of questioning the core of your existence. But remember this: you are not alone, you have never been and never will be. Don't feel like you are the only one in the universe who feels like this; that you are the only one who understands what is like. The world is full of people who, like you, see things in a different light, and stress too much about reality, knowing not everything is all right. Like you, they struggle with purpose and meaning, and they beat themselves up thinking they're worthless and insignificant. They are misunderstood and misjudged, and because of that they feel extremely alone. Nothing could be further from the truth, for them and for you. You are worth so much, and you have so much to give. All you need to do is begin, little by little, loving yourself more from the inside. Don't let external sources plague you with criticisms and judgments and doubt. Know yourself and love yourself, and surround yourself with people who will make you better and lift you up, not the other way around. Give yourself your true value. Become the owner and master of your reality and shape it to your desire; don't let others do it for you. It takes effort and practice, but little by little you will get the hang of it, and you will notice how immensely different your life will be.

Plus, it is not all bad. You are also going to have some intense and amazing experiences. That is the way life is, you know; sometimes it gives, sometimes it teaches, and when it gives, it gives you great things. Imagine a huge boat, a cruise ship, sailing through the tranquil waters of the Caribbean on a September night; you and the prettiest girl in the world stand on a balcony, the ocean breeze wrapping you in a cool blanket of air and saltwater. Yep, you will do that, and then you will kiss her, and she will embrace you, and you will paint an unforgettable moment with the brushstrokes of your love. Do you like motorcycles? I know you do! You will feel the wind on your face as you ride a Honda CBR 900 (it's a pretty cool and very fast bike) through the highways of the city, feeling a connection to the road that almost feels surreal, spiritual even. How about feeling the force of gravity pushing you back against the seat of the muscle car you built, all by yourself! I know that right now you take apart some of your toy cars and have a hard time putting them back together, but over time you are going to get a lot better, and although you don't really like getting your hands dirty, you are going to enjoy getting under the hood and making slow things go faster. You are going to sing, and play the drums like you always wanted to, although you should have spent time practicing more (Dancing is another story--not your thing, for sure). Your movie collection will grow. We have these things call "Blu-Rays" now (wait 'til you see the image; you are going to lose your mind) and a TV that hangs on the wall, completely flat! I remember how much you loved going to the movies; the screen so big that you had a hard time seeing all of it at once, the darkness of the theater making you lose sight of what time it was outside. For a while there you were bewildered with the movie projector, and how it could make moving images out of simple light. Oh, and guess what, you are going to escape the imprisonment that the walls of communism built around you, and you are going to live in the greatest country in the world, and meet people from all over the globe, and the best part of all is, that your life has just begun. You have so much more to look forward to.

I honestly don't know what else I can tell you, except for the fact that after everything, you are still here, you are still standing, and you will continue to stand. You are stronger than you think, young man; if there is something that you need to know, it is that. I am very proud of you for your accomplishments, and for the way you look at the world. Don't feel alone because you are the only one who sees things in a certain light; that's what makes you special and unique from everyone else. The world is full of sheep that just follow what they are told, that just incorporate themselves in the ambiguity of the world and die thinking they accomplished much. You will not be like that, and that brings a smile to my face. Continue to think, continue to doubt, continue to search. You will only find the truth within you; you will find your calling and your place after all the pain. Continue to dream, and there will be no limit to how far you will get.

Remember this, it's important: you have one life and you must live it, and the microscopic moments that will bring joy to your heart (you will recognize them as soon as they happen), those are the moments that life is all about. I know you are not one to show much affection, but make the effort to hug Mom, Dad, Grandma and especially Grandpa from time to time. They will appreciate it, and eventually, so will you. Stand tall and straight, keep your head up and don't look down so much; your future is not by your toes. Most importantly, smile. I will see you soon, and together we shall plan our domination of the world.

Yours Truly,

You

CHAPTER 30

Donnie walks impetuously through the halls, at double the normal pace, carrying a stack of books that include the King James Version of the Bible, Darwin's Origin of Species and the Twilight series. He is a lanky young man of some twenty-four years of age, his gown twice the size it should be, swallowing him up. He has an unkempt beard that he refuses to shave, and light, straight hair that almost reaches his shoulders, making him look like a modern version of Christ. Bob has a hard time looking at him, and steers clear of Donnie as much as he possibly can.

"The word is... the word is..." he mumbles as he walks around. His pupils shake from side to side as if they were combing the area for answers. If anyone passes him in the opposite direction, he makes a point to look straight in their eyes and deliver a message that is too important to ignore. "The word is... the word... the word is rebellion... desist, once more, of the root of all evil, the blood of Christ, desist, the word is rebellion, the world now escapes..."

He completes several laps of the floor as his preaching continues, his hands twisting in unnatural directions, the way a robot at Disney's Hall of Presidents would if its programming got corrupted, or if something broke inside. His speech is almost undecipherable, collecting spittle in the corners of his mouth, his breath acrid, his tone desperate. He passes by the lounge and notices me sitting alone, under the flickering lights. He looks at me momentarily, and I do my best to pretend that I don't see him, but it's too late. The stack of books slams on the table. "The word is.... the triangle, the word is the rebellion of the triangle that is God, us and the world..." I sit there, startled, nodding. He connects his index fingers and thumbs, making a triangle with his hand.

"The word is... the triangle, see. God is the top, epitome of delusion and control, God and the word, drowning in ambition, works opposite the spinning of recognition. Us, the balance that gravitationally pulls the puzzle together, then apart. The word is... the word is rebellion." He looks around with desperation. "The word..." He swiftly gets up and picks his books up from the table, almost with superhuman strength. He thinks he's had an epiphany and must tell the world, everyone's lives depend on it. He now has the key that opens the door to salvation and it is up to him to make it known.

"The word... rebellion. Rebellion!" he screams across the lounge, the walls refusing to repeat the nonsense, but having no choice. Everyone is used to Donnie and his madness by now, and they ignore him like they would a fly on the wall - a very outspoken one - and that frustrates him more. He walks to every table, occupied or not.

"Rebellion! Rebellion!"

He starts rushing through the halls, screaming the message at anyone who is close. A couple of new patients, not familiar with Donnie's antics, become startled and run to their rooms. The zombified ones continue their predetermined walks as if he was just an afterthought. He becomes more desperate to spread the word.

"Rebellion! Rebellion!"

"Rebellion! Rebellion!"

No one answers or pays attention.

Lunch time brings along a shot for dessert, and the speed of Donnie's steps dramatically decreases, along with the rest of his world. He now drags his feet through the halls with effort, slightly hunched, having just enough strength to carry his books. His eyelids are halfway shut, his words spaced out, his vision blurred.

"The word... is..."

I see him walking past me and all I see is another zombie. He heads toward his room; the books are too heavy now, and if he drops one, he will refuse to touch it again.

He wakes up a few hours later, still drowsy but revitalized. It is nighttime now. The wheel starts spinning and he begins to remember. "The word is... the word... is... Rebellion!"

He sprints out of the room and resumes evangelizing. "Rebellion! Rebellion!"

He walks by the TV room and notices that it is packed with people watching the basketball game. It's game seven, Curry's last chance to defeat Lebron. It has been one of the most exciting series in the history of basketball. I am sitting in the back row with Devon, like we did that first night. Big Mike and his colleagues are up front, sitting close to the screen, deeply concentrating on the action, hooting and hollering with every great play.

Donnie barges in, now screaming at the top of his lungs, his eyes flickering more than the broken lights, his fists clenched, arms swinging up and down. "Rebellion! The word is rebellion!"

"Donnie, chill out, man." Mike takes his eyes away from the game, approaching him in a delicate but annoyed tone. "Sit down and watch the game with us, but quietly," he adds.

Donnie grows in desperation and is now pacing back and forth in front of the television, making everyone in the room upset. "C'mon, man!" someone is heard saying. "This motherfu..." But Donnie doesn't seem to understand; he is too invested in his own agenda. His pacing gets quicker, his steps get longer. He grabs his head with both hands, almost like he wants to rip it off his body. "Rebellion! Rebellion... the word! The word is Rebellion!"

Big Mike stands up. There is a look in his eyes that alone brings fear; maybe the look that his victims used to see before he would lose control and his temper took over, landing him in the hospital time and time again. The three-hundred-plus-pound man gets in Donnie's face, his breathing double paced, a light sweat shining him up. Donnie stops pacing and makes eye contact with Mike, thinking that his friend is on his side, waiting for him to join him in spreading the word. Someone mutes the TV. An absolute silence covers the room.

"Donnie, I like you," Big Mike says, "but if you don't get out this room right now... you and I are going to have some issues."

Donnie looks at him momentarily, breathing heavily himself, silently. It's the quietest he has been all day. Mike stares him back, not losing track of his shifty eyes, as if they were engaged in the most intense staring contest ever. Donnie gets within inches of Mike's face, takes a deep breath and yells, "Rebellion! The word is..."

By that time Mike's fist is already on its way and connects with Donnie's left cheek before he can finish the sentence. He falls to the floor, and Mike's colleagues jump out of their seats to hold him back. They can barely contain the big man as he mercilessly uses all his strength to follow Donnie to the floor and pound his face once again. Devon starts crying and rocking back and forth on the chair, anxious. Scared and startled myself, I try to hide my distress and hold Devon close to me, offering my protection to make him feel safe.

A pack of male nurses rush in the room and struggle to diffuse the situation. Mike is a very strong man, and when the rage takes over, he is challenging to contain. They are finally able to take him outside and tend to Donnie, who is still on the floor, startled. They tell everyone else to go to their rooms and close the doors until they are advised otherwise. The crackle of a walkie talkie breaks the tension. *What's the status on the TV room?* it asks. *Contained,* it replies. *We are going to need first aid and maybe an x-ray. Get Dr. Murray up here, please.*

I decide that there has been enough action for one night, so I walk Devon over to his room. I then swing by the pharmacy to get the nighttime medicine. With all the adrenaline rushing through my veins, it is going to be very difficult to get some rest tonight.

I stare at the ceiling as Bob sleeps and the medication takes its time to kick in. Donnie's words intrude my thoughts. With nothing else to distract me, I pay attention more carefully.

The triangle, God, the world and us. The delusion of control.

I find his words poetic and somewhat logical in an existential sense. Could it be that we are the ones that fail to understand? Maybe, or maybe I am more troubled than I think I am, and my mind sees things more like Donnie's than I would care to admit.

CHAPTER 31

The halls were eerily empty, the main lights off for some reason, spreading a shadow of darkness throughout the floor. There were a few dim spotlights left behind, taking on the job, but falling significantly short. I stood in the middle of the corridor, about twenty feet away from the big window, wearing the hideous green robe, which I thought I had gotten rid of a long time ago, and hospital socks. The full moon made a confident entrance through the window, perfectly outlining the silhouette of a person standing in front of it, a familiar shape, but one I didn't recognize from within these walls. Based on the slim-fit black suit he seemed to be wearing, the short, well-styled hair and the maybe close-to-six-feet height, I was almost sure it was a man. But I couldn't see his face; he continued looking through the glass, in the direction of the stars.

I felt an unfamiliar attraction to this human being, one that instinctively told me to get closer. There was something inside me that reassured me I needed to learn something, and this was the person to teach me. I began to approach, almost sliding through the freshly waxed floor in the hospital socks. "Hello..." I said, in a wary tone of voice that the empty halls amplified. "Do I know you?"

"I have wondered the same thing lately," the man said with an aura of condescension, his voice deep and sharp, not breaking contact with the sky outside. His hands were interlocked behind his back, his feet perfectly parallel to one another, his shoes perfectly polished, his suit so well fitted that it looked like it was part of him. "Do you know me?"

"Your voice sounds familiar," I said, stretching my neck to the left in a failed attempt at catching a glimpse of his profile. I couldn't decipher where I knew the man from, which was starting to frustrate me, but the unexplained attraction that pulled me to him grew stronger the closer I got. It was a vaguely familiar feeling, a sense of protection, a reassuring loop that kept playing in the center of my chest and dripped down to my stomach, where it branched out to my limbs in intermittent blasts, like firework explosions. It was the feeling of safety that you felt when someone much bigger than you wrapped you in their hands and told you everything was going to be ok, and they told it with such confidence that you didn't hesitate in trusting them completely, feeling irrevocably secure doing so. I knew the sensation because I had felt it a handful of times throughout my life, where I closed my eyes and clenched my hands together, and I poured myself out, my entire self, without the slightest amount of doubt that someone was listening. It wasn't the responses I had gotten in return that reassured me, it was the certainty that I had been given a listening ear by someone who had the power to make it all better, to make it all go away.

That feeling, of course, would eventually fade out over time, when I realized it had all been a smokescreen, a pill we take as little children to protect us from the big bad world out there, the impending doom that inevitably awaits every single one of us. However, having the same sensation in my gut now gave me a much better idea who the character that stood in front of me was, and for a minute I didn't know if I felt scared or curious, or nervous, maybe delirious. But what I did know deep inside me was that I wanted to engage no matter what; it could be my one and only chance.

"You're..."

"Are you sure you are ready to take that guess, young man?" His deep voice bounced off the glass as his breath left a temporary imprint on it. He turned his head slightly to the left to calculate my position with his peripheral vision. "Your entire life beside you, and this is when you are ready to take a shot in the dark?" the voice chuckled. "Your timing has always been shit."

I felt a slice of anger cut straight through me, rooting itself in my intestines and beginning to spread like a virus. "My entire life, beside me?!" I said with disgust, my face crumpled with apprehension. The anger grew the more I thought about the inaccuracy and the fallacy of that contentious statement. "Beside me? No, no, you are wrong. You have never been beside me. Ever."

The man chortled and continued looking outward. His hands dislodged and now went inside his pockets. "You have always been a pretentious little one; you have always thought you are right, that your logic is accurate every single time. All of you, all the same. You are blessed with a slightly-higher-than-normal brain power and you think you are a divine blessing, that everyone should be at your feet, kissing them," he chuckled again. "You're nothing, nothing, you understand... and you know nothing."

His words were piercing and direct, shocking even, but not untrue. As a spoiled and only child, I had always been treated with extra attention, and yes, many times I thought I was better than everyone else, sometimes convinced that my superior intellect was what kept me distant from the rest of them, but who doesn't, right? My biggest problem had been having flexible opinions, being open to change. If I noticed that someone was acting in a way that differed from mine, or saw things in a different light, I was immediately sure that they were doing something wrong; that they were idiots for looking at things in such a foolish way. Very seldom did I pause to think about the possibility that I was the one who was headed in the wrong direction, and that I should think about learning something from them instead. My instinctive arrogance led me astray, and it was that very same arrogance that now built up inside me, as I encountered the mystery man's audacious statement.

"I know nothing? I know nothing?!" I yelled. "Well, tell me, sir, if you have always been beside me, tell me what you really know about me. Tell me how many times I cried myself to sleep begging you for help, how many times I told you that I couldn't handle it, that I needed you! How many times I was being punched and laughed at and ridiculed, scared, terrified sometimes, anxious about waking up and having to do it all over again, time after time. I didn't even ask you to save me, all I asked you was for the strength to get through it, for the strength to fight back. How many times did I ask you for support to help me battle these demons, to help me get rid of this monster, while I was ruining my life and the lives of all the ones around me? Mom and Dad did not deserve this! SHE did not deserve it!" I fell to my knees, sobbing, almost hyperventilating.

"I didn't deserve this...."

A deep silence settled in for a while after that, the sound of my heavy breathing the only thing that was breaking it. He kept looking up at the stars, as if they would give him the answers on what he needed to say next. Then his head lowered and he now looked at the floor, pointing the tip of his shoe upwards and studying it. "You have made a profound mistake, my friend, your entire life, a mistake that in your position is easy to be made. You have always confused love for comfort, for safety, for protection. How could you not? It is all you've known, the overprotectiveness that left you defenseless against a world that doesn't give a shit about you."

"I am not here to protect you, Jay. I am here to teach you."

The night sky was starting to make the transition into morning when I, still on my knees, looked up to notice a few coy sunrays penetrate the glass and shine around the man's silhouette, highlighting the high quality of his suit, which seemed to feed on the light, absorbing it as if it was a black hole. He looked up in the sun's direction and did not seem at all bothered by the brightness; au contraire, he welcomed it. I became frightened by his presence, having the realization that this whole thing, whatever it was, was much bigger than me; I had to stop thinking in terms of myself but of the whole, the machine that keeps it all going, and then, finding my purpose there.

"Refinement. That is what is all about, Jay. That is what I'm here for. Molding and sculpting, and creating beauty out of tragedy, which is the only way you can create, by the way. There is no place here for pity. It is useless and dangerous; it's not progressive, and this car must keep moving forward. It can't slow down. Get on your feet; stop feeling sorry for yourself. Utilize your power to become who you need to become, and to do what you need to do. Evolve, progress, disrupt."

"What do you want from me; what do you want me to become?" I implored, with tears in my face and deflated voice. "What do I need to do, please..."

My eyes widened and my jaw dropped as the man began to turn around to face me, the red sunlight of the early morning surrounding him, almost making him look as if he was on fire. I gasped as he made eye contact with me for the first time, and I finally understood why he had felt so familiar.

"I want you to be you; that is all you must become," he said, as the sunrays around him became obnoxiously brighter and my eyes shrank for protection, the lights of the room coming to life and the nurse rolling the blood pressure cart through the door. "Checking vitals, fellas, you know the drill," she said, as she gently tapped Bob on the leg a couple of times, knowing he had a hard time waking up.

I sat up on the bed, still gasping for air, trying to come to terms with the intensity of the dream. I had heard that Seroquel sometimes gave people vivid nightmares, but this had felt like so much more. Out of everything, the one thing that shocked me the most was how it ended; seeing for the first time the face I yearned to see for so long, the face I had imagined so many different ways. At first glance, it surprised and even confused me, but after a few moments it made perfect sense. There he was, in all his wisdom, more than I ever fathomed. He spoke truths, as he cannot lie, and he once again did something for me than no one else had: he saw me for who I was.

As his black suit continued to absorb the fire behind him, I had managed to stand up--an arm across my eyes to avoid going blind-- and get face to face with him, no more than a few feet apart. It was then when the image began to dissipate as the nurse turned the lights on in the room, but it had given me enough time to study his face with marvel, and to understand the whole truth.

It was me.

CHAPTER 32

"You have the most perfect woman in the word, now what?"

"Now I am both excited and terrified."

"You now have something to lose."

"Yes, I do. The beginning of our romantic relationship was amazing. We were physically and intellectually compatible, which meant that we thoroughly enjoyed each other, whether we were making love or discussing a philosophy of life. I was completely broke at the time and she was just graduating college, so our dates consisted of microwavable dinners and cuddles on the couch while watching TV. We became enamored with watching entire series on Netflix, most of them in the span of a weekend. The most difficult part was figuring out what to watch next when we were done with the current show. She didn't mind the fact that we couldn't do much outside the house, and neither did I; having her all to myself seemed like the perfect recipe to my happiness. She had the ability to make me feel special and wanted, treasured even. She made me want to become the man that I wasn't but knew I could be. I wanted to give her the world, but I always felt that for her, the world wasn't enough. She deserved so much more.

"After a month or so, I decided it was time to get serious and start planning for our future. I went on Craigslist and found a sales job that would bring a weekly paycheck and the prospect of decent commissions, so we could splurge from time to time on a trip outside the city, or a fancy dinner at that Italian place she loved so much, or whatever else we came up with spontaneously. I could even move up in the company if I did well, maybe become manager someday, cementing a strong foundation for our life together. She began working part-time as a receptionist at a law office, wanting to contribute a little herself. Six months later we rented our own place, a small one-bedroom apartment on the north side of the city. It wasn't much to look at and we barely had any furniture, but it felt ours, it felt like home. Her parents, although apprehensive about their little girl leaving them, bought us a bed, and Mom gave us the old couch and recliner that lived in the Florida room. I bought a small table and four chairs at a pawn shop and took the TV that was in my old bedroom. That was it, that was all we had, but it was more than enough for us."

"How were you *really* feeling?"

"My fear had completely taken over and it was seriously affecting me. I was anxious from the time I woke up to the time I went to bed. There was a voice in the back of my head, constantly asking me what could go wrong that would take it all away, telling me I couldn't handle it, that I couldn't keep things going well, that eventually I would screw it all up. The anxiety became unbearable, torturing me day in and day out. I barely slept, and when I did I would have horrible nightmares. I woke up every day exhausted, in a pool of my own sweat, shaking, so nauseous that I would sometimes throw up. Getting dressed to go to work was an arduous job; just thinking about facing the world out there made everything worse, and I had to handle it all while trying to keep her from knowing what was going on.

"Addiction is like a parasite that feeds on our fears and insecurities, and it grew bigger and stronger inside me every single day. I started drinking before work again, just so I could make it through the day. I would usually have a small bottle of Skyy vodka in the center console of the car, and every morning I would pass by a gas station, get some Gatorade or Red Bull (depending on how hung over I was from the day before) and have a cocktail for breakfast as I drove. Work became a blur; I could never remember what I had done the day before, who I had talked to or what deals I had closed. Sometimes I would fall asleep at my desk, and Martin, who sat beside me, would discreetly shove me to wake me up. *'You have to get your shit together, man,'* he would angrily whisper. *'You're going to get us both fired!'* After regaining consciousness, I would just keep ticking, like a wind-up monkey, just enough to remain slightly functional.

"When work was over I would pass by the store and get one or two six-packs of beer, depending on how much stress I had accumulated throughout the day. One of them would be gone before I even made it home. I would then stumble in the house and throw myself on the recliner, conscious enough to continue working on six-pack number two. The TV would be on but I was too wasted to even comprehend what I was watching. I was living in the purgatory of a world that was neither real or fantasy, but I didn't care; I wasn't in pain, I wasn't afraid and the world wasn't all coming down on me with full strength. She would get home a couple of hours later, and by that time I was so obliterated I could not put two decent sentences together. Initially she would get settled in and sit beside me, and stroke my hair and say sweet things, trying to convince me to move to the bed. Some days I was too gone to even move, so she would somehow tuck herself under my arm and sleep on the recliner with me. The next day the story repeated itself all over again. Day in, day out, the same dread, the same useless existence.

"For the first few months she didn't say I word; she just tended to me as best as she could. I guess she hoped it was just a phase, a fleeting time of wallowing in self-pity brought on by the stresses of so many changes in so little time. At least that's what I am sure she told herself when the alarm clock went off every morning and she would have to do it all over again. But when I eventually lost my job and she found herself carrying the entire load (without me even attempting to help), she couldn't hold it anymore, and her silence ended.

"She told me that she was very worried, but that she loved me and she needed me. She got on her knees and, with tears falling down her face, she begged over and over again for me to get help. 'Whatever you need to do, I'll be there,' she said. 'But just do it, Jay, just get it done and let's move on.' I dismissed the whole thing and told her I was ok; I didn't need any help, it was just a rough patch that would eventually come to an end. She made me promise that I would stop, and if I did, she wouldn't ask for more. And I did, I promised, but deep inside I wasn't trying to prepare for a life of sobriety, I was trying to figure out how to continue doing what I was doing without her finding out.

"While she was at work I was at home, pretending to look for jobs, while in reality, I was crossing the street to the gas station and stocking up on cheap wine and beer. The plan was to get buzzed enough to get through the day, then collect all the empty cans and bottles and throw them out before she got home. Just in case she came earlier than I expected, I would lock the door from the inside so I would have time to hide the evidence in the closet and not get caught. That would also give me time to thoroughly brush my teeth and chew on a couple of sticks of cinnamon gum. It worked for a couple of days, but the day I passed out on the recliner and she found herself locked out of her own home, the cat was out of the bag. She knocked fiercely for thirty minutes straight, yelling my name in tears, thinking something bad had happened to me. The neighbors came out, startled, trying to figure out what was going on. They eventually called the fire department, who came and knocked the door down. To her embarrassment, I was passed out on the floor, surrounded by a bevy of empty cans. Even then I didn't wake up; it was already nighttime when I came to my senses and found her sitting next to me on the bed, crying so loud that it scared me. That day haunts me to this very moment; the sense of guilt that I felt is hard to put into words. But the parasite inside me was too big by then; guilt wasn't going to kill it, not at this stage of the game.

"She didn't give up though; she kept begging until I reluctantly agreed to see my family doctor, just to make her happy. *Melancholy doesn't get treated at the doctor*, I had always been told, and I didn't have any plans to stop drinking. I still thought I could find a way to do it discreetly without affecting her. Heck of a delusion. When I finally saw the doctor, I just gave him a half-assed version of what was going on, and he gave me the only half-assed diagnosis he could come up with, based on what little I had given him to work with. He prescribed half a milligram of Xanax a day to help me cope with the severe anxiety that I clearly had, advised me to go see a therapist and, I quote, to 'get my shit together.' A couple of hours later a pharmacist handed me a bottle with 30 small, orange oblong tablets with the number G3720 imprinted on them. I was curious to find out if this pill could really help with the some of the issues I was having, but more than anything, I was curious to know if it would make me high, and if I mixed it with alcohol how much better the buzz would be. As soon as I got home I popped open the bottle and put four pills in my mouth, thinking that if one would relax me, four would be a good starting point for getting a little toasty. Thirty minutes later, I started to feel it, hard."

"What did it make you feel?"

"Peace, an absurd sense of peace, one I had never felt, not even with alcohol. My heart rate declined and the childhood memories of loss and fear and sadness became so distant I could barely see them or relate to them. My present fears and anxieties were gone, insignificant, silly and illogical. I was confident, I was happy, I felt I had the power to do anything I wanted to, and I wanted to do a lot. There was a constant stream of warmth that birthed in my stomach and radiated to my limbs and head. It felt like I had fountain of serenity filling the emptiest places of my soul, and it felt incredible. Just like that, all my problems, gone. All I needed to do now was find a way to feel like this all the time, and I would then truly be at peace. Another gargantuan delusion.

"I later realized that all the doctor had done was give me a pharmaceutical replacement for alcohol, one that gave me a better high, didn't give me a hangover, and formed a physical dependence that would ruin my life and could potentially turn deadly. What the hell was he thinking?

"In three days, I had gone through the whole pill bottle, not once thinking about the fact that I couldn't go to the convenience store and get more, like I did with alcohol. I now had to resort to new and creative ways of getting my fix, and that was when the scheming and the lies began. When I told her that I ran out of medicine, she questioned me, concerned. I explained that I had opened the bottle on top of the toilet right before jumping in the shower, and well, she knew how clumsy I was. The bottle jumped out of my hand, slimy as an oyster, and all its contents ended in the water. I had no choice but to flush them all away. She bought it, but barely. The doctor was not as gullible, however, and said *no way* when I asked for a refill. My desperation grew quickly, my hunger for mental disconnect almost intolerable. When she went to sleep that night, I stayed up and started scouring the 'Net for options. A couple of shady message boards directed me to an even shadier website, which promised to send me a batch of pills from Canada without the need for prescriptions, and although doing an online drug deal somewhat concerned me, the reward would hopefully outweigh the risk. We had just scraped together the rent money for that month, and I didn't hesitate in investing half of it in the completely unknown. I could deal with the consequences later. In a span of a few days, Xanax had not only become my priority; it had become the only thing I cared for.

"The first package arrived in a week, with four hundred .5 mg pills. Four hundred. They were shipped in a sealed generic vitamin B bottle. It was perfect. I remember dumping the entire contents of the bottle on the bed, getting an intense jolt just looking at so many pills, just there, perfectly orange, begging to be enjoyed. Man... even thinking about it now, I don't know, it's like it activates a part of my brain that has an untamed thirst for them, one that will always be there, no matter what.

"That batch was gone in a couple of weeks, and, for the most part, so was my mind. Taking close to 10mg of alprazolam a day would not only make me completely black out, it would also turn me into the most obnoxious, erratic, careless and violent individual on the planet. My eyes looked demented and my speech would become slurred. I could barely walk and had no rational decision-making ability whatsoever. In a desperate attempt to show me how bad I was getting, she would record me with her phone when I was at my worst, mumbling and screaming, drooling and falling on the floor. When I came back to reality, she would try to make me watch the path of destruction I had left behind, but I couldn't bear it. I always refused to watch and accept the existence of the monster I turned into. I didn't want to know, I didn't want to feel, I didn't want to care, I didn't want to be made accountable for anything. My only goal and reason for living became getting as many Xanax pills as I could, ingesting them as quickly as possible, and repeating the process all over again.

"I began using cocaine about six months later to counter the drowsiness of the pills and to enjoy the high a little longer and also because for whatever reason I craved it every time I got high. I had tried coke at parties when I was younger, and I always enjoyed the rush it gave me, but I had never been a habitual user. I didn't know any coke dealers, didn't even know anyone who would know a coke dealer, so I found myself driving to some of the sketchiest parts of town, trying to score with whatever little money I had, sometimes with no money at all, high and belligerent, barely coherent. Needless to say, it didn't always go well. I got robbed a few times, once at gunpoint. I got beat up a couple of others, not having money to pay for the deal. The craziest part was that sometimes my memory was so choppy I couldn't really make out where I had been, what I had done, or what had happened to me. My rock bottom was reaching a new low.

"This type of habit, of course, requires money, a lot of it, and with her being the sole provider, we were barely making ends meet as it was. She had been able to go from part time to full time hours at work, but that wasn't close to enough. Sobriety, however, was not an option. Every time I ran out of pills the depression would hit me a hundred-fold, and the pain forced me to do the unimaginable in order to fund my habit. I started to pawn every single item of value we possessed; I sold them for whatever cash I could get. She would come home to an emptier apartment every night; no more TV, or laptop, or newly purchased surround sound system. I tried selling the bed, but it was too heavy for me to carry by myself. DVDs and Blu-Rays gone. The convection oven – a gift from her best friend – gone. The Fossil Watch she had gifted me on our six-month anniversary, gone. The one that really hurt her, though, was when I broke into her jewelry box and sold the gold bracelet her mom had given her when she was little. It was a piece of jewelry that had been passed down from generations, to her from her mother, to her mother from her grandmother, and so on. Six generations of women in the family had owned it. That one changed her. She cried a lot that day, - so much that I was afraid she would faint - but not with sadness. Only tears of anger fell to the floor that day.

"When I ran out of my and her things to sell, I had no choice but to begin stealing from my parents. When they left for work, I would use my key to sneak into the house and go through all the drawers, taking anything that I could turn into a buck; watches, chains, earrings, antiques... anything. They always pretended they hadn't noticed, but I knew they had. When I was high I really didn't care, but when I wasn't, it filled me with a preposterous sense of guilt that I could barely withstand.

"We eventually got evicted from our apartment after not being able to pay the rent. Her dad refused to get us out of another jam, having done it way too many times already. That day, when he saw us standing outside with the few belongings we had left, he got out of the car yelling expletives, making a stabbing motion with his index finger. If she hadn't gotten between us I'm pretty sure he would've punched me. He had grown a very distinct type of hatred toward me, one so deeply rooted that I am sure it will be there, in his bones, long after he dies. He saw me as the epitome of a useless human being and man, not able to provide for his family or even respect himself. The fact that his precious daughter was with such an atrocity broke him inside in more ways than one.

"We moved into my childhood bedroom with my parents, and she wasn't thrilled, not one bit. She was exhausted, defeated, numb. I think she had lost sense of who she was, and why she was doing it all. But there she stood, by my side, for longer than I thought, more than I expected her to. She made an extraordinary effort to understand and endure, and I will always be appreciative of that."

"How long?"

"Two years. Two years of carnage that annihilated anything and everything that surrounded me. I don't remember much of that time, but I do know that it left us, especially her, emotionally scarred, in a way that no other problem could have. Our relationship deteriorated quickly; we barely spoke to each other anymore. We hadn't had sex in months; we no longer enjoyed it. She looked at me with disgust when I would climb on top of her, and I could barely perform anyway. I would sit alone on the recliner for hours, while she locked herself in the bedroom, usually crying. I remember laughing when I heard her sobs through the walls. In my inebriated state, it was funny to me that she would be so upset about something so silly. *Who cares, right? Who needs her! As long as I have my pills, everything is going to be ok...*

"That day, I was sitting in our bed nursing the usual daze, excited about dumping on the bed the new batch of pills that had just arrived in the mail. The routine was always the same: I would count each and every one of them to make sure they were all there, and as I started consuming I would continue counting them; it brought me a certain sense of security to know that I had enough medicine to take care of me for the next few days. But as the number started diminishing, I would begin to get anxious, and that's when I would resort to the usual repulsive behavior in order to get more.

"That day she sat on the floor, in the corner of the room, knees bent toward her face, sobbing and shaking as I ingested an inordinate number of pills. Her pain was just an unfortunate casualty of getting what I needed, and when I was high, I couldn't even empathize. I felt nothing. What I hadn't realized up to that point was that my addiction wasn't only taking the fear and the pain and the anxiety away, it was also taking the love, the compassion and the common sense. It was leaving me a shell of a man.

"That day was when she finally gathered the courage to look up at me and, in between sobs, say, *I'm sorry, I cannot do this anymore.*'"

"Jay... are you ok?"

"Sorry. I really don't want to talk about this anymore."

"We can stop there for today..."

"I never, never intended to hurt her…"

"I can see that. However, trying to run away from reality always brings pain, suffering, and, worst of all, regret."

"I didn't see that back then. I couldn't."

"Do you see it now?"

"In excruciatingly vivid detail."

"The only difference between the way we judge ourselves and others is that we don't make excuses for others."

CHAPTER 33

I walked in the room feeling disheartened about the therapy session. I sat on a corner of the bed as my eyes drifted toward the window, chasing the light. My mind kept replaying the story I had just shared with the doctor, a dark part of my life I had never confronted before. I was now face to face with the reality of my actions, and the guilt that I had suppressed for such a long time was roaming free through my veins. My chest constricted and I found it difficult to breathe. My eyes welled; the ringing in my ear became constant and gradually louder. Short flashes of memories stabbed me in the back as if they were seeking long-awaited revenge. I wept. I wept so hard that I had to cover my mouth with the pillow to muffle the cries. Everything came at once, and after a while, it disappeared. I became surprisingly calm, my thoughts cleared like the clouds do when the rain stops, the pressure on my chest lightened, my hands relaxed. It was almost as if I had confronted the monster, starved it and expelled it from inside. The light shined through the window, the specks danced. That was when I realized that Bob's shelf was empty, his belongings now tucked away in the small carry-on bag that stood by the door.

I ran out of the room to find him, fearing that if I didn't I wouldn't get to see him again. I went to the TV room and the classroom. I peeked into the examination room and swung by the big window. I finally found him at the nurse's station, in the company of a social worker, signing some papers. After a couple of signatures on the dotted lines, he shook the man's hand and sat down at one of the tables in the lounge, opened his Bible and began to read. He wasn't smiling, but I could tell he was happy. Even his face was honest in showing his true emotions.

I rushed over to give him what I thought needed to be a much-deserved scolding. "Well, you kept this to yourself, Mr. Bob. I thought we were better friends than that."

"Calm down," he smiled. "I just found out this morning while you were still with Dr. Patel, *sharing feelings*," he said, making air quotes with his hands and putting on a sarcastic frown.

"Funny," I said. "I gotta tell you, Bob, I'm very happy that you are getting out of here, but I definitely hate to see you go."

"I know!" he grinned. "Who knows who they are going to give you as a roommate now!"

I lowered my head with genuine concern. I hadn't even thought of that particular detail. "God..." I said. "I just truly hope he doesn't pee himself at night..." That comment produced a nostalgic smile in Bob, instantly reminding him of his good friend, Jerry.

He now looked at me, like a worried father looks at his troubled child. "How are you holding up, Jay? Are you going to be ok?"

"I want to go home, Bob. I want to go home really bad..." I said, trying to not let my voice crack, nor my spirit.

"I know the feeling," Bob replied. "You are almost there, kid. Stick it out for a little longer and get your mind and your meds right. Follow through and get it done; you won't regret it."

"I don't know if I can do this, Bob. I truly don't know if I can. The therapy session earlier broke me, and reminded me of how screwed up I really am. I feel like I am stuck in a deep well and there is no rope to lift me out."

Bob looked down at the table. There it was, his trusted Bible, the one the he always relied on to give good advice. He reached for it, to most likely base what he was about to say on one of his "go-to" passages, but his hand stopped shy of it. He looked at the leather cover momentarily, as if asking for forgiveness, knowing that this time it was best to speak directly from the heart. "Do you know what the difference is between the way we judge ourselves and the way we judge others, Jay?"

"What?" I asked.

"We don't make excuses for others," he replied.

His answer pierced like a perfectly shot arrow, right in the heart. What he said made perfect sense.

"Don't make excuses for yourself," he continued. "You are bright enough and capable enough to find your true path in life. You are a bright kid, I can tell, and you have a great heart. Just what you did with Tara showed me how great you really are. You have amazing potential, Jay. Don't waste the opportunity you have been given in life."

Opportunity, I thought. *He is the second person that has talked to me about opportunity this week. It can't be a coincidence, can it?*

"Bob... I am not very good with words, and much less with feelings," I said. "I... I don't know how to thank you... you know... for being there."

"You don't have to thank me," he smiled with a tenderness I hadn't seen from him before. "It's just what friends do." He stood up and extended his hand. I shook it firmly, knowing he liked a strong handshake. He reached over and hugged me, tighter than I expected, giving me a couple of pats in the back. I didn't have anything to give him as a farewell gift, so I left a couple of tears imprinted on his shirt. I looked him in the eyes and he looked back at mine. "Godspeed, Jay," he said.

"Godspeed, my friend. May God always look after you as you deserve."

His wife called at around two in the afternoon to let them know she was downstairs, waiting. He grabbed the small carry-on bag by the handle and went around shaking hands with most nurses, who had accumulated a deep sense of respect for him. A couple of lucid patients also said goodbye, but not as many as the ones that came to see Jerry go (Bob wasn't as charitable with his time). The plastic wheels of the luggage made a distinct sound as they rolled down the hall and toward the double doors. One of the nurses swiped the card and pushed the button, and the doors gradually opened outward, allowing Bob re-entry into the real world.

I never saw him again, but often thought of him and what he did for me. It'd be a hot summer day, not too humid, a light breeze curiously traveling between the foliage. Bob would be camped under an oak tree, enjoying the cloudless blue sky, the cool flow of air and the imposing shade of the old tree. His wife would have a picnic blanket by their feet, filled with an array of snacks, sandwiches and drinks. Out in the open pasture, the girls would throw a frisbee back and forth, chortling when the frisbee went rogue and they had to chase after it. His wife would lay her head on his lap as he read his Bible, glasses halfway down his nose, in his usual style. He would be deeply focused on the book of Job, his favorite passage. It would remind him of all those people he met at Memorial Hospital that time, when he found himself being tested, but never abandoned. He would remember me and smile, knowing I was out there somewhere, confident I had adhered to his advice of not wasting the opportunity. From time to time he would look away from the words and soak it all in, feeling blessed, thankful and proud of his accomplishments. He would let the breeze caress his face and make him feel alive, then return to his reading.

Every time I found myself in the midst of a tough decision or a precarious situation, Bob's voice would pop in my head and caringly advise me, just like he did that day. When I listened, things had a way of working themselves out much better than I had thought. In that sense, he always stayed with me, always cared for me, always reassured me that there was a better way. He was always a true friend. I became a better person with a simple concept that Bob taught me that day I reached out to him when I woke up to Tara on my bed:

Everyone deserves a chance, and in order to succeed in life, I needed to give myself one.

CHAPTER 34

There was a tall behemoth of a man with unusually big hands sitting in the middle of a circle of chairs in the TV room. He sported an overweight physique, a piece of his belly peeking through a t-shirt that would be too small in another ten or fifteen pounds. The curls of his hair – a mix of blonde sprinkled with some gray – rained carelessly halfway down his ears. He looked like a bodybuilder who was forced to retire by the passing of time and the natural demise of the human body. His hands rested on his bulging belly, fingers interlocked in what I assumed was a link impossible to pull apart.

"Please sit wherever you'd like," he said as I walked in. He kept looking down at his hands, his eyes following the shape from the fingertips to the huge palms that could probably swat and kill a baby elephant. He then unlocked his fingers and curled them, carefully studying the perfectly trimmed nails. He gave a sly smile, obviously proud of a genetic advantage very few people were fortunate to have. A very peculiar man, he was.

I sat across the circle from him and he did not say another word to me. As more patients walked in, the pre-recorded greeting would play over: "Please sit wherever you'd like... please sit wherever you'd like..." He didn't even notice when all the chairs were occupied, so focused on himself he had been the whole time. "Please sit wherever you'd li... oh, I guess we are all here. All right then, let's begin.

"My name is Hans and I will be conducting this process group today... welcome. Pretty straightforward stuff; we are going to be sharing some of our feelings, processing through some of our issues and hopefully feeling a little better. Everyone is welcome to share and there is no topic off the table. However, I do request that we respect each other and treat each other kindly, no questions asked. Who would like to start?"

Hands began to raise, slowly at first, a little quicker after everyone got acclimated, and Hans began to call on the participants one by one. Some of the issues being discussed felt silly at times. Some of the patients had difficulty expressing their feelings, communicating with others, taking their medications, finishing their food. Others had obsessions that drove them mad; cleaning up after themselves constantly, and then after others (whether they wanted them to or not), having to count every step they took (if they miscounted, not only having to start over, but backtracking to where they began), having to brush their teeth every 30 minutes no matter what (which led to severe gum bleeds), and so on. It is challenging at first to empathize with problems that you have never experienced, to put yourself in their place and live their nightmare. But after a few minutes of seeing how deeply their issues affect them, you realize it's not about the problem itself, but about the damage it has on their day-to-day life. Then you can make the connection, having problems in your life that affect you the exact same way.

Big Mike vented about his challenges with anger, and his lack of emotional control when he gets mad. He felt very guilty about what happened with Donnie and wanted to apologize, but didn't know how. His eyes showed sincere remorse. For the first time, I witnessed the crooked eye lady talk to someone that I saw as well. She spoke calmly and articulately, not even the shadow of the woman I saw roaming the halls, sometimes half naked and tormented. The medication she was on would sometimes work great, sometimes not so much. Sometimes the voices would order her not to take it, and if she obeyed, the darkness would take hold of her. She gave a traumatizing depiction of how much terror the voices put her through, and it was more horrific than I originally thought. I felt a severe case of desperate empathy for her, having the desire to do something to help her, but knowing there I was nothing I could do. One can feed the hungry, give shelter to the homeless and protect the abused, but no can help you escape the torment that stems from inside your own mind. Donna the diabetic ranted angrily about the mystery person that continued to steal her biscuits, and how someone had to do something about such transgression. When she was nicely confronted by another patient about the serious risks associated with her actions, she had an answer that muted the entire room: "I want to die like I live, happy, and ain't no one gonna take that away from me. I won't let them."

Filling a chair in the circle of twenty or so was a new patient named Shelly, restless and a bit neurotic when she spoke. When she had her chance to share, she began to yell about the travesty of her forced hospitalization, and how her husband, who was a Navy Seal, would tear the whole place apart when he found out where she was. She beamed with sweat and her hands shook, almost like she had drunk one too many cups of coffee, or had snorted a few lines of coke. Her voice was loud and deep; if there had been a wall between me and her, and all I could hear was her voice, I would have thought it was a man. Her eyes shifted rapidly from side to side, so fast that I'm sure she didn't have the ability to focus on anything specific. Her tone was so aggressive that a couple of patients who were sensitive to loud noises left the room, trying to hold back the panic. When she finished the tirade, no one dared offer any input, and the big man just moved on to the next person. Hans never gave his own opinion; he just listened and gave permission to speak, more like a mediator would. When Donna went on a second rant about the biscuits, he had to interrupt and reprimand the voice that yelled, "You just need to stop being a fat bitch!" Things got more heated when someone came to Donna's defense. "You shut your mouth, you disgruntled prick!" But Hans was well prepared and knew how to quickly diffuse the tension and maintain control of the room. He was less useless than I initially thought. Once the room was again quiet, he scanned the circle and, like a lucky spin on the Wheel of Fortune, landed on me. "Jay, would you like to share?"

No, of course I don't want to share! I had a tough enough time sharing with Dr. Patel, and that was just in the awkward intimacy of a one-on-one session. I especially didn't want to share in this malfunctioning circle of trust. I began to open my mouth to politely decline, and before a word came out of it, another voice interrupted.

"I would like to share."

"Go ahead, Tara," Hans said.

I had not heard her speak in such a mellow tone before. Just like the crooked-eye lady, Tara was surprising me with her unusual demeanor. "Hello, my name is Tara. I am 28 years old. I was born in Tennessee, some time ago. My mom and dad were young and couldn't afford to raise me, so I lived with my aunt until I was 12. She was an angry lady, not nice at all. She would get drunk every other day and beat me, sometimes for hours. She had these rods and she liked the way they swooshed through the air as she was hitting me... she would laugh the louder I cried and the more I bled. If I said something that slightly annoyed her, she would force me to eat these sandwiches that she would make with rotten meat. I would get sick all the time. One time she got so mad that she walked down to the basement, and spent at least an hour searching for the biggest roach she could find. Once she did she came up to me and squeezed my nose shut, and when I gasped for air she shoved the whole thing down my throat. I threw up all over the kitchen floor and she beat me until I ate the throw up off the floor. She got so tired of the fact that I kept vomiting back up that she hit me so hard she broke my arm. When I went to the hospital I had to lie and tell them I had fallen running, but they noticed the rest of my bruises and took me away for good. She went to jail and I went into foster care. I lived for a while with this family that had two other boys. The parents were nice. The older boy took special interest in me, which I liked, at first. Then his interest grew with each passing day, and he got progressively meaner... he raped me every day until I was fifteen. Then it was to another foster home, where I would lose food privileges for every silly thing I did. I was really thin back then. After high school, I left home and lived in the streets for a while. That's when I met Hayato. He used to work the counter at the gas station in front of the park where I slept, and he would give me cans of baked beans when I had nothing else to eat. I immediately fell in love with him and he with me; I didn't care that his wife and his friends didn't like me. He loved me and I loved him... He loved me and I loved him. It was his wife who called the cops when she found me hiding in the basement of the store, and she told them that I had sneaked in at night through a window, and when she told me to get out I had threatened to kill myself, and I had stabbed myself in the arm, and that I tried to choke myself, which were all lies! She told the cops I had been hiding there for days, and that I was the one who was harassing her husband, and that he was scared! That was when they brought me here, and here I've been…" she looked up at her audience, a couple of big tears attempting to leave her eyes. "My point is… why can't people just be nice… like Hayato… or Jay! Thanks for letting me share."

The room went quiet. There was a sob from someone who could relate well to sections of her story, and a few sympathy tears from others. Donna, who sat to Tara's left, tenderly looked at her and delicately rubbed her back, a motherly action at soothing a child. Shelly forgot about her previous qualms, and was now furious at the helplessness she felt listening to Tara's account. Her eyes shifted rapidly as if trying to find a solution for Tara's problems somewhere in the room. The crooked-eye lady, in a moment of profound emotion, got up and dragged her feet over to Tara, momentarily piquing everyone's curiosity. She bent down and hugged her tight, but no words were said. A painful smile and a tear came out of Tara's face. There was an intense silence that brush-stroked the scene of one of the most powerful moments that I have ever been a part of; the moment where all barriers are broken, and the limitations of our minds and crippled bodies are erased, leaving nothing but pure humanity, naked and transparent, fueled by the most primal instinct that connects us all: love.

"Thank you for that, Tara; we appreciate it," Hans said, as he quickly scanned the circle again. "This has been great, excellent… Jay, back to you, are you going to share?"

CHAPTER 35

"Let's talk about what happened the past couple of weeks," Dr. Patel requested. My parents were sitting beside me, Mom with a visible look of apprehension, Dad protecting himself with his arms, trying to show no emotion. This was going to be the toughest session of all, I knew that. But if I got through it, I would most likely feel ready, and get the doctor's blessing to go home.

"Well... ahem..." I stuttered and squirmed in my chair. I glanced over at my parents, who now had their heads down and were holding hands. They looked like they were sitting on an airplane that was falling from the sky, bracing for impact. I looked at Dr. Patel, who gave me a nod of approval, letting me know it was ok to proceed.

"She had left the house and went to live with her parents about four months ago. Even though I was devastated, I had the faint hope that we could work it out somehow, that I could fix things. I begged and promised that if she gave me just one more opportunity, I would do anything she wanted me to. I would go on those long walks she enjoyed having after a stressful day at work, when the dying sun would stroke the sky a reddish hue, and the trees welcomed the afternoon breeze. I would learn how to dance a little better, so I could eventually take her to sweat a few nights away. I would never be as good as she'd want me to, but she would appreciate the effort. I would ignore my strange aversion to bubble baths, jump in the tub with her and give her a nice massage, surrounded by candles. Most importantly, I would go wherever I needed to get the right help; any doctor or therapist or guru, and this time I would be completely honest. I would do it all if I had to."

"What was her response?" Dr. Patel asked.

"She wasn't sure," I replied. "She felt like she had been broken beyond repair. She said something inside her snapped and she didn't see me the same; she couldn't trust me. She couldn't see a future with me anymore.

Mom sniffled and wiped a few tears from her cheek.

"I still thought that if I stayed close enough I could prove to her that I was changing, that I was gradually getting better. I could try to win back her trust, I could grow back her love. I used all opportunities at my disposal to see her, whether at church, or sometimes catching her as she left her place of work. I wanted to prove that there was still potential, that what I saw in us never died; it just withered in the face of adversity. She was nothing more than polite when she saw me, but she no longer showed emotion--no distress, no love, just raw indifference--and that hurt even more. But even after all that, I still had hope. I didn't want to give up on her. I couldn't.

"Two weeks ago... I received a call." My hands began to tremble. I pushed them harder against my thighs so no one would notice. "She said that she wanted me to hear it from her before I heard it from anyone else. She said it had been the toughest years of her life and that she knew she deserved better, and she wanted more. She said that she had given me priority all this time and tried to do everything in her power to be there for me. She said that it was time to now put herself first, and that's what she would do. Jaw-man came back into her life and she was giving him another chance. Later I discovered that he never left; he was the shoulder she had been crying on while we were going through our struggles. It was probably him who had given her the strength she needed to endure longer. He waited patiently to get back what he thought was rightfully his, and I gave it to him on a silver platter."

"How did that make you feel?"

"Numb at first, then betrayed, then I felt like the most incompetent, incapable and irrelevant human being on the planet. None of the pain or sadness that I had felt throughout my life, not even through the worst depressive episodes, had hurt this much. I felt that I wasn't worthy of the air I was breathing, that I didn't deserve to be alive. I felt that the labor pains that my mother went through to give birth to me had been for no reason, that I should have..." then it hit me. "I felt... like Job."

Mom sobbed. Dad broke down in tears. They held each other tighter. "I ordered six hundred pills online, overnight shipping. I scanned my parents' medicine cabinets and found some Vicodin, left over from Dad's wisdom teeth surgery. I crushed those and snorted them while I waited for the package to get to me. The rest I only remember in sections, and not very clearly. I remember walking a long distance to the area where I usually found some coke, but I honestly don't remember if I did or not, although the blood tests would say so. Then I remember getting on my knees and begging God to kill me. Then there was yelling, crying and fear. I remember the knife in my hand and Dad battling me for it, then falling to my knees and screaming as hard as I possibly could, leaving my throat sore and dry, and having no more tears to cry. Mom fell on top of me and held me, while Dad paced back and forth in the kitchen, grabbing the hairs in his head, panicking. That was it. Once the chaos was somewhat in control I ended up in the emergency room of Memorial Hospital. I had no idea that two weeks had passed, to me it felt like a few hours."

"Thank you, Jay," said the doctor. "I think your parents know, as well as I do, that what you just did takes an incredible amount of courage, and I feel comfortable saying in behalf of all of us, that we greatly appreciate the effort." She gave me a hint of a smile and then directed the attention to my parents, who were both in tears. "Could you please share your version of what happened those days?"

In all the years that I had been dealing with these issues, I had never heard my parents talk about them in front of anyone, especially me. They had never even gathered the strength to do an intervention; they were too afraid to tackle the issue head-on, hoping that prayer and hope would fix it somehow, without them getting in the way. Too late had they realized that things didn't work that way, not with addiction, not with mental illness. But I gave them a lot of credit for acknowledging their mistake, and their willingness to do whatever it took to get me better. That was all they wanted in the end.

The world again shifted down and started to slip away from my hands, everything in slow motion and blurred, their voices distant. Everything moved sluggishly, everything but me. I saw my mother's lips articulating, her eyes red and her tears plentiful. I saw Dad put his hand around her shoulder and squeeze, his go-to move to let Mom know that he was there, with her, every step of the way. I saw Dr. Patel ask, and they answered. I sat there motionless through the passage of a story that belonged to me, but wasn't mine. This was their story, their pain, their regret. This was the sleepless nights I never knew about, the constant crying, the relentless worry. This was the acceptance of the fact that their child could die way before they did. This was the feeling of helplessness that constantly haunted them. This was their lives, their most important responsibility a massive failure, rendering them legally useless as parents and human beings. I sat there, carrying the heavy burden of affecting those lives - the lives of the most important people to me - and of destroying so many things. I knew that even if I got better one day and became an exemplary human being and son, the regret of what I had put them through would get to rest beside to me in the grave.

Almost like switching on a light, the world regained its normal speed and I was now sitting in Dr. Patel's office, alone. "That was very productive, I must say," she said. "I now feel comfortable in giving you an accurate diagnosis."

I felt a flutter of nervousness shoot up my back. I took a deep breath and anchored myself to the seat. "Go on…"

"When I initially took hold of your chart, I was very inclined to diagnose you as Bipolar II. Some of the symptoms fit the illness well; the recklessness, the periods of sadness since you were a child. But what I have heard from you and your family is that your bouts of erratic behavior don't stem directly from your personality, but from

201

the substances you use to self-medicate. I can tell you for a fact that you have a depressive and anxiety disorder. Your brain does not produce enough serotonin and that leads to a chemical imbalance that affects your mood. I also think you have had a hard time throughout your life dealing with serious issues because you were never taught how. Your parents' overprotectiveness and fear hurt you more than it helped. You developed a serious depressive condition that remained untreated until now, and you were doing whatever you could to keep the pain at bay. There is childhood trauma also; not dealing with your grandfather's sudden departure, being bullied and rejected at school. There is a lot you haven't dealt with, Jay, and it has piled up over the years. You are going to have to continue seeking counsel for your addiction; I will recommend a couple of rehab centers. You need to keep taking the Librium and tapering down to avoid another withdrawal episode. I am keeping you on the Effexor and Seroquel since you seem to be doing well with them. You also need to see a psychiatrist on a regular basis who can continue to prescribe you the meds and monitor you. I will make a couple of recommendations for you as well. Even though I can't completely rule out Bipolar disorder, I think this is the best and most accurate a diagnosis as I can give you, Jay, in the short time that you've been my patient."

"That sounds like decent news, like something that can be treated…" I said, surprised.

"It is as good news as I can possibly give you. You have a chance to get your things straight and have a good outlook on your future," she smiled. "Don't waste it."

"What now?" I asked.

"You tell me," she responded.

"I would like to go home."

She looked down at the chart, picked up a pen, wrote a few notes and went to the last page. She scribbled what I imagined was her signature. The folder slammed shut.

"You are going home."

CHAPTER 36

I sat under the flickering lights, having one last supper in the presence of the broken clock. Oliver had been wheeled out of his room and sat by the nurse's station, listening to a small radio behind the counter that gave the play-by-play of a baseball game. Donnie sat two tables away from me, reading a book at his accustomed speed and taking notes with the usual urgency. His left eye was still a dark shade of purple from when Mike had punched him. He was whispering in between breaths, so quickly that it sounded like the hum of a bumblebee. The crooked-eye lady, zombified, dragged her feet across the hall. It was difficult to conceive that this was the same woman who had spoken so eloquently at the process group, the woman who had shown such empathy and concern for another human being, and even got up and made that emotion known by giving Tara a caring hug. That's how I wanted to remember her; that's how she deserved to be remembered, like her true self. She would no longer be the crooked-eye lady to me, she would be… and then I remembered. When she had raised her hand to share, Hans had to ask her, "And you are, young lady?"

"Rachel," she said. That's how I would remember Rachel, the awesome-hearted lady.

I looked up at the clock and smiled. *I have enjoyed our chats, but it is time; I'm getting out.* It had been a week but it felt like years. I had grown and learned so much the past few days that I felt like a different man, a better man. Now that I had a better understanding of my condition, I knew what I had to do to better manage it. I was, for the first time in a while, thankful, that I had been able to gain some traction on the slippery slope that was my life, and I now had a more positive outlook on the future. I sat at the table for a while and lost track of time. It didn't matter anymore; I was no longer desperate to walk through the double doors. I wanted to absorb the surroundings, making sure that I saved a good mental image of everything. I wish I'd had a phone or a camera, so I could have taken pictures of Tara and Tony and Bob, and my good friend Devon, and Callie. Their faces were clear as spring water in my head now, but I knew that through the years they would start withering away, becoming more of a blur. I felt sad thinking about it, knowing that I would probably never see them again; life trajectories that for some of them, like Tara and Devon, would always revolve around places like this one, and medications and doctors and shots. Not the life they were meant for. I felt guilty, having to leave them here so I could try to live a normal life if I wanted to. How come I had a choice and they didn't? What made me any better than them? The thought made me angry and bitter, but then I thought about Devon's smile, and it brought me peace.

The social worker briefly stopped by, had me sign a few discharge papers and gave me a few rehab recommendations, as well as a month's worth of scripts, signed by Dr. Patel. I then went to the room to pack whatever few belongings I had so I would be ready when the time came. As I walked in, I noticed a young man lying on the bed that had previously belonged to Bob. He wasn't older than twenty-five, a blonde-haired, blue-eyed former high school jock and prom king, I'm sure. He was wearing a white tank top that was sprinkled in dry blood and on his wrist, a red bracelet. His body was thin but muscular, no doubt that he played some sort of sport. *This kid had it all*, I thought to myself, pretending to know his life story. It's what we all do, we become judges and critics and prophets without a hint of evidence, barely scratching the surface. *Who knows what he has gone through, the nightmare that he has lived*. He sat up on the bed as I walked in, apprehensive, bathed in fear and despair, not knowing who I was or why I was there.

"What's up, man? I'm Jay," I said, extending my hand.

"Shawn," he responded shyly.

"Don't worry, Shawn," I smiled, hoping to put him at ease. "It could be worse. I'm getting out soon but before I do I will try to get you acquainted with the program. Oh, and before I forget, and this is important... Careful with the little one."

It was Sunday morning. I took a quick shower and studied myself in the mirror as I put on a favorite: my brown leather jacket. I had refused to wear it before, no matter how cold it got on the psychiatric floor. No, the best clothes were always reserved for Sundays. For a while I stood in front of the mirror, looking into my eyes, exploring them well. The shatterproof mirrors were made of what I think was some sort of aluminum, opaque and blurry, not at all like a real mirror. Still, I looked deep, wanting to know why they looked different, what filled them up. It was then when I noticed something I hadn't seen before, not ever.

Possibility.

I walked over to the big window. The sun was bright and the clouds distant, the blue expansion touched everything in sight. The usual hustle and bustle of the freeway was in full action. The offices below were empty, closed for the weekend. All those people were probably out there, on the freeway, heading to Clearwater beach for a nice dip and a tan, soaking in the impressive view that the bridges gave them on the way there. They would be with their significant others, maybe their kids, maybe just a few friends. What I was sure of was that they weren't alone; they were with someone who enjoyed their company, who cared about them. They were the most fortunate people in the world and they didn't even know it. I looked up and noticed the little birds playfully chasing each other again, chirping and singing with great contentment. *They came to say goodbye*, I smiled. *Callie would have loved it. I hope she's doing well.*

A nurse escorted me to the locker room to get the rest of my stuff. Then I went and lay in bed for a while, wanting to gaze at the stars one last time. I woke up an hour later, realizing that for the first time I had been able to get some good sleep without the aid of any drug.

When I looked out the door, I noticed Devon and Tara standing out there, waiting for me. She waved her hand in elation and Devon smiled.

"We heard you were leaving," Tara said. "Didn't want you to go without saying goodbye." Her honest and caring display of affection moved me. Devon extended his hand and handed me a white sheet of paper and a small pencil. "Phone," he said.

"Sure!" I smiled. "Just make sure you call me, ok?"

"Can I have your number too?" Tara asked.

"You make sure to stay in contact too!" I told her, as I ripped the paper in two and wrote my phone number on each half.

Devon smiled from ear-to-ear, with his intoxicatingly pure and distinctive smile. *It will be hard to forget that smile, no matter how much time passes.*

Tara hugged me and squeezed me almost as hard as the first time. "Gonna miss you, Jay," she said as she held on to my waist. Then I realized, *Damn, I'm going to miss you too, Tara.*

A nurse escorted me toward the big double doors. As I walked past the lounge I did one last scan of the psychiatric floor. Oliver still sat in his chair by the nurse's station, daydreaming of a sunny day at Wrigley field. Donna walked around, again with her gown open, not a care in the world. She seemed to have found some of her precious biscuits, and looked ecstatic. Devon sat at a table, drawing more calendars. I wondered for whom this time. Tara chased down the director to give him her latest report. He made an attempt to ignore her, but he should have known by now, Tara was impossible to ignore. Mike and Donnie sat together again, in the usual fashion; Donnie ranting and Mike playing with his hair, their altercation left in the distant past. It was nice to see them together again. The crooked-eye... no, Rachel, sped past me in tears, trying to get away from the impossible to escape. I looked away. *That is not how I will remember her.* William sat at a table by himself, lost in thought, trying to reconstruct his past, one blurry memory at a time. I caught a glimpse of Maggie hiding behind a column, able to tell that her eyes followed me. I made brief eye contact, smiled and waved my hand goodbye, but she just stood there, petrified, like a statue. Then I saw her hand quickly wave, and, just like that, she disappeared. I absorbed the scene, all at once, and my eyes got moist, my heart ached. The broken clock slowed everything down for me one last time, and a voice penetrated the back of my head.

Like sheep without a shepherd.

The card was scanned and the button was pushed. The big double doors swung open like the wings of the mother that knows it is time for the fledgling to leave the nest, and once again, I regained full access to the real world.

* * *

"Ten years ago, I had one of the most profound experiences of my life, one that served as the foundation to a significant shift, from a path of self-destruction to a path of healing. It was just the beginning of a long road ahead, difficult at times, but worth it in the end. I attribute a lot of my progress to the work that Dr. Patel initially did with me, because she took the time and effort to get to *understand* me, and not only medicate me. Unfortunately, many, if not most, psychiatric healthcare professionals do not take this approach today, and they are not only failing the system, they are also failing their patients. The Mental Health field has made significant progress through the years, but it still has work to do, and we must begin by taking the same approach with all patients that Dr. Patel did with me. We must care.

"I also attribute a lot of my personal growth to the people I met there, like Tara, Devon, Jerry, Bob and Callie. They taught me that even the most flawed individuals can have amazing hearts and can influence your life in ways you thought impossible. They taught me that we are all flawed in different ways, and the smallest variations of our imperfections make us remarkably unique and incredibly special.

I carry them with me everywhere I go, and I often speak of them, because they deserve to have a voice, and I feel it is my personal responsibility and my duty to make it so. I give them credit for many of my changes, including my sobriety. They showed me my worth, they taught me that I could accomplish so much, and in their honor, that is what I try to do. I think that people like them need more recognition, support and, like Tara would say, compassion."

The circle broke in momentary applause. A voice said, "Thank you, Jay, what a wonderful story. We have been thoroughly moved by your words today. Congratulations on ten years of sobriety. We wish you success on a lifetime of clean living."

I looked around at the faces in the circle. The morning sunlight that came from the window started to slowly dissipate, as if the sun itself was dying. Suddenly the lights in the room also turned off, and for a moment I was blind. When they came back on, the faces were gone, and the room had morphed. I was now in the TV room of the psychiatric floor. Tara and Devon sat next to me. Bob sat in the chair in front of me, reading his Bible, glasses halfway down his nose. Callie was by the window, daydreaming, looking at the playful birds. Her skin seemed to glow with the sunlight; her eyes were bluer than ever. Donnie stood quietly by the board wearing a modern suit, solving a dense equation. Donna walked in, wearing a beautiful red gown, twirling in happiness, with a biscuit in her hand. Tara calmly ate mixed fruits from the plate on her lap. Devon smiled. Jerry and Oliver whispered jokes in each other's ears, and they laughed. Oliver's eyes were no longer murky; they were dark brown and full of life. Maggie sang, her voice sweet and pure, and Alexandre applauded her. William rocked a baby girl back and forth in his arms, singing a lullaby, a caring smile on his lips. She wore the prettiest tiara on her head, just like her mother's, who was standing by them. Rachel walked in, dressed in a gray pantsuit, her hair styled and groomed, her glasses hiding her slightly crooked eye. She greeted everyone, and everyone greeted her back with smiles, happy to see her.

The lights went off and on again, and I found myself surrounded by the original circle. I felt slightly disoriented and a little nauseous. My heart gave me a light tug, my eyes moistened. *I haven't forgotten... I haven't forgotten their faces; they are still there, clear as spring water.* I grinned. Someone spoke.

"Would anyone else like to share?"

ABOUT THE AUTHOR

Jay Chirino is a recovering addict, mental health advocate and writer, living in Tampa, FL, with his family.

Made in the USA
Lexington, KY
03 January 2019